O9-AID-471

Moment of TRUTH

Books by Kasie West

Pivot Point
Split Second

The Distance Between Us
On the Fence
The Fill-In Boyfriend
P.S. I Like You
By Your Side
Lucky in Love
Love, Life, and the List
Listen to Your Heart

Moment
of
TRUTH

KASIE WEST

HARPER TEEN
An Imprint of HarperCollinsPublishers

HarperTeen is an imprint of HarperCollins Publishers.

Moment of Truth
Copyright © 2020 by Kasie West
All rights reserved. Printed in the United States of America.
No part of this book may be used or reproduced in any manner
whatsoever without written permission except in the case of brief
quotations embodied in critical articles and reviews. For information
address HarperCollins Children's Books, a division of HarperCollins
Publishers, 195 Broadway, New York, NY 10007.
www.epicreads.com

Library of Congress Control Number: 2019946116
ISBN 978-0-06-267581-1

Typography by Torborg Davern
20 21 22 23 24   PC/LSCH   10 9 8 7 6 5 4 3 2 1
❖
First Edition

To my soul mate sister, Stephanie Ryan. Love you!

ONE

I moved my arms in a windmill as I stared out over the pool in front of me. The water had calmed from the last race and the still night made it look like glass. I couldn't wait to break through its surface. I rotated my head side to side to the beat of the music blasting through my headphones. My music was loud but I sensed a hush come over the watching crowd. That wasn't normal. I brought my brows together, determined not to think about it. I needed to stay in the zone. No distractions.

The shrill sound of microphone feedback cut through my music. I tugged out a single earbud and looked up.

The first thing I saw was my dad. He sat in the middle of the bleachers with a goofy grin on his face. He waved. Mom was next to him, typing something into her phone.

The feedback sounded again and then someone cleared their throat into the microphone. The noise wasn't coming from the booth, where the announcer was looking around, just as confused as the crowd.

"Ladies and gentlemen," the voice said. "May I present Heath Hall."

"What the—?" I mumbled. "No."

A low buzz of chatter rippled through the audience.

"The guy from the movies?" someone behind me asked. "Is he here?"

I knew the real Heath Hall wasn't here. Well, obviously. Heath Hall was a spy hero character played by the actor Grant James. But the person about to appear was neither the character nor the actor. The person about to appear was some attention-seeker who I'd successfully ignored until this point.

The coaches and officials moved around the pool, searching for the interruption. That's when a guy in a Speedo and rash guard emerged from the locker room across the way, hands in the air. He was wearing a Heath Hall mask. Not one of those cheap, plastic, fake-looking masks but a high-quality, very realistic version of Heath Hall encased his head. The same exact mask I'd seen in online pictures classmates had posted over the years of him causing public disturbances. If I were closer I would've seen the electronic eyepiece and scar running along his right cheek that some mask maker had painted on so we wouldn't mistake this mask for another one of Grant James's characters.

The impersonator let out a guttural yell and charged straight for the pool. My mouth dropped open. The coaches rounded the pool but weren't fast enough to catch him before he jumped in feetfirst. The voice over the rogue microphone said, "Go, go, go!"

The crowd soon joined in as fake Heath Hall swam the length of the pool and crawled out right next to my starting block, mask still concealing his entire head. He gave me a thumbs-up, water flicking off his hand and onto my arm, then took off at full speed toward the open gate. I wiped off my arm and watched the coaches attempt to catch him. He was too fast. A few moments later they walked back, defeated.

"Okay," the real announcer said. "That was interesting. Are we ready for an actual race? One hundred free, take your places."

What? No. My chest tightened in a panic. My goggles were still pushed up onto my forehead, very much not in place. The other racers were heading toward the starting blocks. I swallowed my protests about needing more time, realizing none of the officials seemed to care, then quickly tugged out my other earbud, dropped it on top of my parka at my feet, and pulled down my goggles, pressing them into place.

Less than thirty seconds later I dived into the pool. I was glad this was my last heat of the night; my body was tense. The lines on the bottom of the pool were there just like they always were, but as I fell into my rhythm, the image of the guy wearing a Heath Hall mask seemed to take over my vision.

Stop, I told my brain.

My shoulders burned and my eyes stung with the pain. I winced and pushed through, forcing my arms to make the rotation even though they tried to tell me as loud as possible that they didn't want to. I touched the wall and then flip-kicked off it. Just one more length of the pool. The adrenaline masked some of the pain. I stretched out and with one final kick, touched the wall.

My eyes went straight to the results board. I was three seconds slower than my normal time, putting me in fourth place. I hit the water in frustration. It was the first race I'd lost in weeks.

Coach stood over my lane so I pulled off my cap and goggles.

"Hadley, how are the shoulders?"

"Okay."

He raised his eyebrows. "Go have DJ ice them." Coach reached down and gave me a hand out of the pool. He didn't say anything else. He didn't have to.

After rinsing off in the shower and pulling on my T-shirt and sweats over my still-wet suit, I went to the trainer's office.

DJ sat in a chair, his feet on the desk, reading a book. There were some who faked injuries just to get in front of him. His dark eyes were so concerned as he'd check out any ailment. And yes, he was cute. I wasn't interested, but I wasn't blind either. With his light brown eyes and loose dark curls he looked like the sweet best friend in movies who always ended up with the girl.

I knocked on the glass of the open door and he looked up.

"Are you busy?" I asked.

He held up his book but the title was in Spanish so I couldn't read it.

"For school?" I asked.

"Sort of," he said. "And to make my mom happy. Apparently language can be lost in as little as one generation." He set the book aside and sat forward. "What can I do for you?"

"Ice."

He jumped out of his seat. "Shoulders?"

I was only ever in here for one reason: my shoulders. "Yes."

"Come in." His hands were gentle as he guided me to the seat he'd just abandoned. "Your races go okay? You seem upset."

"I'm fine," I said, not wanting to talk about the only race I lost tonight and how irritated I was about the distraction. Apparently my face had already done the talking for me. I changed the subject. "I didn't think you'd be here tonight."

"I'm here so the real trainer can be poolside." He scooped ice into two large ziplock bags. Only half of his last scoop made it into the bag, the rest spilling on the floor. He fumbled with trying to clean it up. I bent down to help him and he waved me off and left it there scattered across the floor. He returned to my side.

"I know you don't take this pain very seriously, Hadley, but if you're not nicer to your shoulders, this could get serious soon. You need to rest them more."

"I'm nice to my shoulders."

He gave a grunt of disagreement and placed a bag on my right shoulder. "Hold this."

I did and he grabbed the plastic wrap, then began to secure it down. As his hands worked their way around my shoulder, his shirt brushed my cheek. It smelled so good that it relaxed me a bit. He moved on to the other shoulder and I looked away to control my urge to sniff him.

"Okay, you're all set."

"Thanks."

"Maybe for a while, until your joint pain settles, you could work on your form."

I smiled. "Yes, Coach."

Amelia, my best friend, was applying mascara when I joined her by the lockers. After she put it back in her bag, she turned and poked one of the ice packs attached to me. "Nice. You're all suited up for some football."

"Funny."

"How was DJ? As dreamy as ever?"

"Yep. Still the cutest nerd I know."

"Do you think he'd date a high school student?" Amelia often set her boy-sights high, determined to land guys that were mostly unavailable to her. I liked her confidence, even though her plans almost never worked.

I always supported her unrealistic hopes because I knew that she knew they were just that. "He only graduated last year, right?" I wasn't exactly sure because he'd gone to a high school across town.

"Yes, but I feel like college years are like dog years

compared to high school years."

I opened my locker and pulled out my towel and bag. "Dog years?"

"Yes, for every year you're in college, you're like seven years older than a high school student."

"You're weird."

"And proud of it."

I opened my bag and stared inside blankly. "Were you out there for my last race or were you already in here?" Amelia swam the race right before mine so she was often changing when I was up.

She scrunched her nose, looking guilty. "I'm sorry, did you want me to watch? Are your parents not here tonight?"

"No, it's not that. Heath Hall was here. He jumped into the pool."

"What? And I missed it?"

"He completely distracted me . . . and probably all the swimmers."

"That sucks. So . . . did you get a good look? Who is he?"

"What?"

"That's the online debate. He's obviously someone from around here because most of his public appearances—"

"Public disturbances," I interrupted.

"Have happened within, like, a hundred-mile radius."

"How do you know this?"

She turned one way and then the other as she looked at herself in the long mirror on the inside door of her locker. "Someone did a map of them."

"People have too much time on their hands."

She shut her locker and leaned her back against it. "By the way, did I ever tell you that my brother met the real Heath Hall last year? I mean the guy who plays him—Grant James."

I rolled my eyes. "Yes, only a million times."

"That's because it's cool! And Grant James is hot."

I shoved my towel into my bag and zipped it up. "Is that what Cooper said?"

"Yes, actually, he did. Was this guy hot?"

"What? No, I mean, I don't know, he was wearing a mask."

Her eyes went wide. "Just a mask?"

"Yes, just a mask." I shoved her shoulder. "No! He had on a Speedo and a rash guard too."

"So . . . did he have a nice body?"

"I don't know. I wasn't paying attention. He jumped into my pool!"

Amelia raised her eyebrows. "*Your* pool?"

"Well, my lane, whatever. He spread his bad mojo all over it."

She laughed and slung her backpack over one shoulder. "You and your rituals."

"I don't have rituals, I have routines." Routines that made me win races and today that routine was wrecked by a wannabe Heath Hall. If I ever found out who he was, I'd have some words for him.

TWO

Sarah's street was lined with cars when we pulled up after the meet. "I thought you meant this was a party for just the swim team," I said, peeling the ice packs off my shoulders, the numbness not completely hiding the ache.

"That's what I thought she meant. I guess a few more people showed up."

I dumped the ice into the gutter and left the empty bags on the passenger-side floor. I didn't go to a lot . . . okay, any . . . real parties. I hadn't even changed. I was still in my suit and sweats. Amelia looked adorable next to me, makeup and all. I self-consciously tugged at my still-damp hair and tried to smooth it into place.

We walked through Sarah's house and into the back-yard, where the majority of people were. Sarah lived in a neighborhood built around a man-made lake. In the middle of that lake, a large island, complete with lamps and picnic tables, had drawn everyone's attention. Or at least that's what several people were pointing at—the island. They chanted something I couldn't quite make out. Someone's name. I scanned the island but didn't see anything out of the ordinary.

"What's going on?" I asked as we came to a girl at the back of the crowd.

She gave me a double take, surprised to see me here or surprised my hair was wet; it could've been either. "They're trying to make him swim out there," she answered.

"Why?" This wasn't a swimming kind of lake. It was full of fish and who knew what the neighborhood kids threw in. It wasn't very deep: a lake people used paddle-boats on and took engagement pictures in front of. It wasn't practical. It was for looks. Plus, that island was at least six pool lengths away.

"They dared him."

"Who?"

"I'm not sure. I just got here."

"What does he win if he does it?"

Amelia elbowed me. "Don't even think about it."

"I'm already in my swim stuff."

"Hadley wants to do it!" the girl we'd been talking to screamed.

I rolled my eyes. I hadn't said anything of the sort. But soon the whole party was chanting *my* name and my heart started beating to the rhythm.

"You haven't even heard what the prize is," Amelia reminded me. She must've seen how my eyes lit up at the possibility of a challenge. And it would be a challenge. My shoulders were already shot.

I pushed through the people until I came to the front of the group. Jackson Holt was toeing the water with his bare foot. "You want to race me, Moore?"

I groaned and almost walked away. Jackson was one of my least favorite people ever. He was so . . . middle school. Once, in the cafeteria, he pretended to be hurt just so Mindy Halpburn, who happened to be walking by, would stop and help him. When she realized it was a joke, she slapped him and the whole room laughed. And this wasn't even the most childish thing he'd ever done. Yet everyone seemed to love him, in the way they loved puppy videos or chocolate—they couldn't get enough.

Those thoughts kept me from fleeing. Maybe it was time to humble Jackson a bit. Make him realize he didn't always have to be the center of attention, loved by all. He wasn't an athlete. I could win a swimming race against him easy, sore shoulders or not.

"Are you sure you're okay being beaten by a girl?" I said softly.

He stripped off his shirt, his toned chest making me think twice about his athletic abilities, and jumped in, jeans and all. When he surfaced, a playful gleam shone in his eyes. The gleam that shone there most of the time. "The water's great."

I stepped out of my shoes, then eyed the island. Did I really need to do this? My skin buzzed to life, telling me I did, in fact, need to do this. I pulled off my sweats and waded into the water beside Jackson. Unlike the school pool, which was heated, the chill of the lake immediately sucked the air from my lungs. The water smelled like mud, fish, and mildew. I almost got back out.

"Can't pass up a competition, can you?"

Someone standing above us called, "On your mark, get set, go."

I took off, not knowing if Jackson followed. Not really caring. My shoulders ached a bit, but I didn't press them and the more I swam the more they loosened up. It was weird swimming in silence. I was used to having my music on for everything but races. It gave me a rhythm to swim to and kept my head clear of unwanted memories.

About halfway through the swim, I felt a movement by my foot and then suddenly it was yanked backward. I went under for a second and came up coughing. Jackson treaded water next to me. It was nearly black in the middle of the lake, but I could see his teeth glowing with a smile. He smiled way too much.

"I thought you were going to try, Moore. Make this hard on me."

"What?"

"I thought you were on the swim team."

I coughed again and wondered what the best way to dunk him would be.

"Lighten up. I was kidding. I could barely keep up with you. Couldn't you give me a tiny break?"

It was only then I noticed him panting for breath. "Oh."

"And I'm tired. I thought I was going to drown out here in the middle of nowhere and you'd be all the way to the island, leaving me with no help."

His smile made it hard to tell if he was still kidding or not.

"That was the last chance I had to make a grab at your foot before you were gone." He looked down at the water, his head bobbing with his movements.

The people back on the shore looked as tiny as insects.

The island was closer. If he really was having trouble swimming, the island was where we needed to go.

"I think I can make it," he said, probably noticing my analysis. "Do you think there are fish out here? I'm kind of scared of fish. At least there aren't any sharks. Do you swim in the ocean a lot?"

"Rarely," I said. Even though we lived within a five-minute drive of the Pacific, the waves didn't mimic my race conditions so I didn't practice there much.

"If . . ." His eyes got wide, then he looked down again.

"What?"

"Did you feel that?"

"No."

"It must've been noth—" He went down fast, under the water, and out of sight.

I gasped, then reached forward, feeling around for him. I dived under, but between the murky water and the dark night, I couldn't see a thing. I surfaced and propelled myself in a circle, panicked. The people back on shore couldn't hear me through their loud music as I yelled for them. I gave up and continued to search around me.

A full minute later, Jackson broke the surface fifty feet closer to the island. "I think I'm going to beat you." With those words he began to swim.

My heart turned from beating in fear to beating in

rage. I couldn't believe I fell for that after I had just reminded myself what he had done to Mindy in the cafeteria. "You are the biggest jerk," I called. But he acted like he couldn't hear me as he closed the distance to the island. I thought about turning back to shore but then I wouldn't get to pummel him with no witnesses.

With a kick of my feet, I took off.

By the time I got there, Jackson had dragged himself onto the island and sat on one of the benches—his wet jeans making puddles below him. Hopping out of the lake, I lunged at him, punching him on the shoulder several times.

"It was the only way I could win." He grabbed my fists, laughing.

"You are such a jerk. I thought you drowned." I relaxed my arms and he let go of my hands.

"It's nice to know you care."

I hit him one more time for good measure, then plopped on the bench next to him.

He looked me up and down. "Do you wear your swimsuit everywhere you go, just in case someone calls for a race?"

"We had a meet tonight." I looked at my bare feet, feeling a bit stupid now. Why *had* I done this? "What do we win for doing this dare anyway?"

"Win? What do you mean?"

I sighed. Now that the adrenaline was gone, the ache in my shoulders returned. I took in the distance back to shore.

"You think someone would come rescue us with a paddleboat if we yelled loud enough?" he asked.

"I think they lost interest." Everyone back on shore was jumping around, dancing. My stomach let out a gurgle, reminding me that I hadn't eaten after my races.

Jackson must've heard the sound because he said, "Should we start a fire? I can catch a fish."

"We'll swim back. Just give me a minute."

"Most people find me amusing," he seemed to say to himself.

I stood, shook out my legs, and rotated my arms a few times. "Have you ever heard of the boy who cried wolf?" I asked.

"You think there are wolves on this island?"

"You fooled me once. I won't fall for it again. I hope you can swim back." With that I dived into the water, leaving him alone on the small island with his dripping wet jeans.

"The boy in the story got three chances," he called after me.

When I reached the grassy backyard again, Amelia stood at the shoreline, holding a bag of chips. "I wondered when you'd be back. Was it worth it?"

"No." I wrung out my hair.

"So there was no making out with Jackson Holt?"

"What? Gross."

"Really? You don't find him cute? I think he's cute."
She crunched into a chip.

"You think everyone is."

She started to protest through her mouthful but then
said, "True, but he really is."

"He might be cute but it's hard to tell through all
the annoying." I snatched a chip out of her hand and
bit into it.

"Annoying? Huh. I think he's funny."

"Interesting. He thinks he's funny too."

She laughed. "So I was talking to Katie while you and
Jackson were making out."

"You and Jackson should hang out. You both think
you're funnier than you are."

She hooked her arm in mine and led me away from
the water, ignoring my comment. "And she said Heath
Hall is not just from *around* here; he actually goes to our
school."

It took me a couple seconds to catch up with her train
of thought.

"The masked man," she prompted.

"*Fake* Heath Hall," I said. "So who is he?"

She shrugged. "That's part of the mystery."

"Mystery?" I stopped at the now-empty space of ground my clothes used to occupy. "Where are my clothes?"

She led me to a chair, where they were folded nicely. I pulled my shirt on, then stepped into my sweats.

"Yeah, he's all over the internet, but nobody knows who he actually is. Or at least nobody is outing him."

"If nobody knows who he is, then how does Katie know he goes to our school?"

"Rumors, I guess."

"I need food," I said, nodding to her chips. "Where did you get those?"

Amelia pointed, and we headed toward tables covered in pizza boxes and snacks set up on the patio. "So are you curious?" she asked.

"That guy made me lose my first race in weeks. So yes, very curious."

THREE

I awoke to a persistent knocking and let out a moan. "Yeah?"

The door swung open. Mom poked her head in. "You're still asleep?"

I wasn't sure if she wanted me to answer that question or if she was making a statement, so I rubbed my eyes and sat up. My shoulders protested.

"Hadley. You have thirty minutes."

My mind, slow from sleep, tried to play catch-up.

My struggle must've shown on my face because she added, "It's the fifth. Of April."

"Oh!" Eric's day. Crap. I hopped out of bed, tripping over the sheet that had tried to follow me. I'd seen my dad charging the car battery the day before. I couldn't believe I hadn't connected the two. "I'll be ready."

She gave me the look that showed she was hurt. I had forgotten and she was hurt. I was a horrible daughter. "I'm sorry." I kissed her cheek and ran for the bathroom. To make up for oversleeping, I'd have to skip the shower. My shoulders weren't happy about that plan. They needed some heat therapy. I hoped gross lake hair wouldn't be doubly offensive to my mom. I brushed my teeth, pulled on some clothes, and ran to the corner mart near our house. I searched the aisles until I found Eric's favorite candy: Hot Tamales. I paid and made it back to the house just in time to see my dad stepping down from the porch.

He smiled. "You ready?"

I wondered if my mom had told him I'd forgotten. I clutched the bag with candy. "Of course."

"Then let's do this."

"Where's Mom?"

"She's coming." He led me the fifty steps to the truck that sat on a raised platform under our big eucalyptus tree in the front yard. The place it had sat for the entire sixteen years of my life—a monument to my brother who died before I was born. Our front yard was big, but the truck seemed larger than life today.

My dad patted the hood. I could see the emotion in his eyes. I felt nothing. I mean, I felt bad, of course, because I hated seeing my parents so sad. As for my brother, his dying so young was tragic. But I hadn't known him. I knew *about* him. The things my mother had told me over the years. The things my parents said on this day every year. But still, I didn't know him. My dry eyes seemed to taunt me. Why couldn't I just conjure up some tears for my parents this year? The tears that had come naturally when I was younger. I knew I didn't care less now, so what had changed?

I stared at the cab of the truck—the keys dangling in the ignition. My dad must've come out earlier to make sure everything was in place.

"Do you want to start her up this year?" my dad asked, probably noticing where my gaze lingered.

My heart jumped. "What? No. That's your job."

"This year you actually have your license. Maybe it should be yours from now on." He put an arm around my neck. "In fact, maybe this year we should sell her and get you your own car."

The beating of my heart doubled. My own car. "Really?"

"I think it's a good idea."

I bit my lip, trying to contain the smile, but then

my heart rate slowed as his eyes ran the length of the 1955 light green Chevy truck, taking in each perfectly restored part. It really was a beautiful truck. Probably the only reason our neighbors tolerated it sitting on our lawn for so long—it was like a piece of art. My heart knew it was an empty promise. My parents wouldn't sell the truck even though we only started it once a year. And I wouldn't want them to.

"You think what's a good idea?" my mom asked, carrying a box and joining us.

"I was just telling Hadley that we need to get her a car of her own. Maybe it's time to sell the truck."

"You're going to sell your truck? Then what would you drive?"

"No. Not my truck," he said softly.

It took her a long moment, but her eyes widened when she finally realized what he was implying. "Eric's?"

"We're not selling it," I said quickly. "It was just a passing thought. We'd never sell it. I'm fine."

My mom's face relaxed, but my dad let out a heavy sigh.

I nudged him with my elbow and forced a smile. "Well, go on. See if she starts."

He gave me a sad half smile, then climbed onto the platform and into the cab. He looked at his watch. Without needing to check the time, I knew it was now exactly

8:23. The time my brother had taken his last breath. Dad held up crossed fingers and turned the key. It rumbled to life, just like it did every single year.

My mom opened the cardboard box she held as my dad climbed down. The purring engine became the background noise for our mini memorial service. "Eighteen years ago Eric lost his battle with leukemia. Today I brought a few things to remember him by." She reached into the box and pulled out a movie. "This was his favorite."

I squinted to read the title. *The Hunt for Red October.* I'd never seen it before.

"He loved spy movies," Mom said.

It surprised me that year after year she could come up with new things about him. I didn't think she'd ever repeated herself. Never used the same memory twice. My palm started to sweat where it gripped the shopping bag. The Hot Tamales seemed so stupid now. My mom had brought the candy just last year.

The next thing she pulled out of the box was a water gun. "He was a jokester. He loved to hide out sometimes and surprise me when I rounded the corner." She laughed a little. It was an odd thought—my mom getting pelted with a water gun. I couldn't even imagine her reaction. Then again my brother had gotten the younger version of my parents. Now they were in their late fifties, graying hair and wrinkles in place. I wondered if they'd been more laid-back then. Either way, I wouldn't dream of squirting any version of my mom with a water gun. I, apparently, was not a jokester.

"And last, I brought a picture of Eric with Julie at his junior prom. Do you remember this, Daniel?" She showed my dad first and he smiled.

"The funny thing about it was that just thirty minutes before this picture he was covered head to toe in grease from working on his truck all day. He cleaned up nice." My dad showed me the picture.

I could see a little of myself in my brother. We had the same auburn hair and the same freckled skin. But he got my mom's green eyes where I got my dad's brown. I stared at the picture, wanting to know the stranger looking back at me. Wanting to know what it would have felt like to have an older brother. But again, I felt nothing.

My mom replaced the picture in the box and shut the lid, then walked to the truck. She removed the box from last year, tucking it under her arm, and reverently set the new one in the passenger seat, where it would sit for a year. I wondered what my mom would put in a box like that for me. What things she would choose to highlight in my life. I wasn't sure she knew me as well as she knew my brother.

To end our ceremony, she exited the truck and placed a single hand on the hood. "You will forever be remembered and forever be missed."

My dad nodded his head toward the bag I clutched. "Did you have something to add, Hadley?"

"Oh. No. I'm good." I quickly touched the hood, then took two steps back.

My dad patted the hood as well. "We miss you, kid." Then with a few quick steps he was back in the cab, turning off the ignition.

My mom hugged me, tears in her eyes. Then she pulled away and retreated into the house. Probably to make our annual meal—Eric's favorite.

Back in my room, I clicked on my music, dug the Hot Tamales out of the bag and stared at the picture of the sunglassed flame speeding across the front of the box. I had never actually tried them before even though my mom had bought them over the years. When I was a kid I had declared my own favorite candy—Twix— and insisted she buy me that every time she bought Hot Tamales. And maybe it had become a habit, but I still hadn't tried them.

I opened the box, poured a handful into my palm, and popped them into my mouth. Ten seconds later I was in the bathroom, scooping water into my mouth. I patted my stinging lips with a towel and dropped the rest of the box in the bathroom trash. It gave a loud clunk as it hit the bottom. Gross.

I wiped my eyes—the heat from the candy producing the first tears of the day, proving my tear ducts were in functioning order. So it was just my heart that wasn't working right. Shouldn't I have felt something, anything, out by that truck today? I sighed.

I took a long, extra hot shower, then pulled on some shorts and a tee. My shoulders gave a dull ache, reminding me of my last race. My computer was open on my desk and I stared at it for a moment before I sat down and powered it on. From friends posting online, I had seen a few pictures of the guy in the mask showing up at events before. But I had never cared enough to care. Never really looked into his accounts.

I pulled up a search engine and typed, "fake Heath Hall" into the bar. Pages and pages of hits about the hero spy movies came up along with pictures of Grant James and his sometimes-girlfriend—actress Amanda Roth. I closed out the tab and went to check social media sites for any information on him. I found lots of fake Heath Hall fan accounts, none of them verified and each only boasting a couple thousand followers. After a while I found the account I was looking for and scanned several pages worth of pictures and posts. But I couldn't find the event map Amelia had been referring to the night before. I shot her off a text: **Hey, where did you find the fake Heath Hall appearance map online?** I still wasn't sure how Katie or anyone else was convinced he went to our school and I wanted to see if the map provided any proof.

She didn't answer back right away. She was probably sleeping. I moved the cursor on the screen to the little envelope icon in the corner, and before I talked myself out of it, I clicked. Once in his DM, I typed a quick message: **Is it your goal to distract people to the point of losing? You are messing with futures.**

My finger lightly rested on the Send key, but as I read the message through three times, I decided it wasn't right. I deleted the two sentences. He obviously didn't care how his antics affected other people. What he really cared about was himself. So instead, I typed: **Stay away from the pool or I'll tell everyone who you really are.**

Sure, I had no idea who he really was, but he didn't know that. I hit Send and went to get myself some breakfast, the taste of Hot Tamales still lingering on the back of my tongue.

The kitchen smelled of bacon, and my mom was dusting the glass box on the wall. She carefully hung Eric's keys back inside the box, not to be touched again until next year.

In the house, that box framing the keys was the only

thing of Eric's we still had. It could've been a lot worse. His room could've still been set up just like he had it. Like he was going to walk back into the house at any moment. It wasn't and I was grateful for that. His room was now my mom's office. I was grateful for that too—that they hadn't put me in his room. I already felt enough like the replacement child sometimes.

As these thoughts streamed through my head, I felt guilty for thinking them. My parents loved me. I forced the thoughts away and grabbed my plate of Eric's favorites.

"I'm going to swim this afternoon. Is that okay or did we have something else planned for today?"

"Coach called for a practice on a Saturday?"

"No. This is just me. No official practice or anything." My stiff shoulders let me know that I needed to work on conditioning them more. Swimming easy, like DJ had suggested, no pressure.

"You don't have any homework?"

"I finished it yesterday during free period."

Her eyes took in my wet hair. "But you just showered."

"I know. I should've waited until after, but I didn't shower last night." I wasn't sure why I didn't tell her about my shoulders, that I had needed the heat and pounding water to help them feel better. Maybe because

I was worried she'd tell me to take a break. I didn't need a break. She wouldn't understand that.

She looked at my hair again as if she was going to tell me no just because I'd showered too soon, but then she said, "That's fine."

"So I can borrow your car?"

"Sure."

I checked my phone as I headed out the door. Amelia hadn't responded to my text and fake Heath Hall hadn't responded to my message. Guess I was playing the waiting game.

FOUR

A shadow fell across my face as I turned my head to breathe. I stopped midstroke and looked up. DJ stood over my lane, gave a small wave, then pushed his black-rimmed glasses up his nose. He often wore contacts, but his glasses made his brown eyes look even bigger.

I pulled out my waterproof earbuds and the music that had been blasting in my head became background noise.

"I thought we agreed you were supposed to take a break from this." DJ said "this" as if swimming was just some sidenote and not my life. "Especially on the weekends. You know there's an entire ocean with waves and sand and people just five minutes away."

I glided to the wall, where I could support myself. "People? You want me to people?"

He smirked. "Is that asking too much?"

I smiled back. "That's not at all what we agreed to. You told me to swim easy. I'm swimming easy."

"I meant take a break occasionally."

"Is that what you're doing? Taking a break?" I gestured back toward his office.

He ducked his head. "I left my book in the office last night."

"Reading. Is that how you people?"

He shrugged and blushed a little. "Um . . . no . . . Well, I just left off right in the middle of an important part."

"Because you had to ice my shoulders?"

"How are they feeling?"

"Really good, actually." And that wasn't a lie. I was flushing out the lactic acid that had built up the night before.

"Good." He lowered himself to the cement and his keys fell out of his pocket. He scooped them up and shoved them back in. "You think Coach is going to let you swim all four races?"

"How do you know about that?" That was my goal. Right now I was swimming three, but I wanted to add butterfly to my race schedule and Coach thought it was too much.

"Everyone who is ever around the pool knows about that, Hadley. You ask him on a weekly basis."

I laughed. It was true. For a second there I thought maybe he and Coach had been talking, maybe he had some inside information.

"Have you had any college interest yet?" he asked.

"I'm scheduled to visit some, but I still have time to decide. I really want San Diego and I really want a swimming scholarship." The coach there had been to several of my races. Adding the butterfly to my schedule might push him to make me an official offer.

"Is that all?"

"I know it's a lot to hope for." I put my arms up on the cement and rested my chin on them, inches away from his legs. My toes clung to the slanted portion of the wall under the water.

"If anyone can get it you can."

"What about you? What are your plans next year?"

"Continue with my undergrad classes for sports medicine. Here in town."

"You're staying here?"

"I'm only eighteen, you know. I do have a lot more time to decide."

I realized it must've sounded like I was judging him.

"I'm sorry. I didn't mean for that to sound like . . . I'm just surprised you want to stay here is all."

"I like it here. You don't?"

"I . . ." I needed to get away from here, away from the ghost that hung over our house. I couldn't say that to him, though. I didn't say that to anyone. "I like it here. I'm just ready for a change."

He smiled. "Change is good."

He held my gaze, seeming to imply something more than what he was saying. I started to ask him another question when he quickly stood. "I better go, let you get back to practice."

"Okay. Have fun reading." That sounded lame but it was too late to take back.

When I climbed out of the pool thirty minutes later, I had a text waiting for me from Amelia: Red Café tonight. I will impart to you everything I know about fake Heath Hall.

After my second shower of the day and a much-needed nap, Amelia and I sat at our usual corner booth at the Red Café. Amelia took a sip of her soda, then offered me some.

"No."

"Still punishing yourself?"

"Not drinking soda is a reward, not a punishment."

"In what universe?"

"It helps my time."

"You say that about everything." Before I could respond she said, "I know, I know. If you don't sacrifice for what you want, you'll be sacrificed."

I laughed. "That's not how the quote goes."

"I like mine better. Or how about this quote: Hadley has more self-control than . . ." She paused and I waited. "I have no idea how to finish that one. It was going to be good, but I couldn't think of anything that has as much self-control as you."

"You make that sound like a bad thing."

"It wouldn't be so bad if it didn't make me look bad."

I picked up my burger. "Hey, I still eat greasy food. I don't have *that* much self-control."

She bumped her burger against mine. "Thank goodness."

Maybe I did need to give up greasy food. That would probably help my time. "So tell me. What do you know about the masked man?"

She held up her finger, finished chewing, then dug her phone out of her pocket. She typed on the screen and turned it toward me. A picture of Heath Hall—dark hair and startlingly blue eyes looked back at me. The electronic glass was lowered over one of his eyes and a long scar came out from under it and down his cheek. "Look." She scrolled down past the pictures and had me read the most recent post.

I read it out loud. "I'll be at the Pacific High swim meet Friday night. Come see what I'll be facing." My eyes went to the post below that. It said, "Bravery makes us all heroes," which was something Heath Hall liked to say in his movies. I rolled my eyes. As if jumping into a swimming pool was equivalent to saving the world.

"Yeah, I saw that when I looked before. He announced it. Who does something like this?"

She shrugged.

"So have you heard any theories about who he is?" I asked.

"Yes, lots. Everyone thinks he's someone different. So he could be anyone at our school."

"Or nobody at our school."

"I guess that's true," she said. "But here's that map of events he's shown up at. It's like a web with our school at its center." She typed something and then showed me her phone again.

"Huh." She was right. The Pacific Ocean spread out along the left side of the map, but the other three directions surrounding our school were littered with red dots, probably close to fifty of them. I zoomed out and noticed another small cluster inland, surrounding a city at least two hours from ours. "But what about these?"

"The theory is he moved from there to here a few

years back." She pointed at the first cluster of dots and then over to our school.

I narrowed my eyes, following her finger. I was irritated there were *any* theories about some random deviant. "Well, all I care about is that he doesn't come to the pool on race day again. I'm going to make sure of that."

"How?"

"I DMed him."

Amelia dropped her hands to the table and turned her wide eyes to me. "What? You did?"

"Yes. I told him to stay away."

"I hear he doesn't respond to DMs. Wait . . . did he actually respond?"

"No."

She waved her hand over my phone that was sitting facedown on the table, bouncing on her seat twice as she did. "See if he's responded now."

I sighed but then wiped my hands on a napkin and picked up my phone. One message waited in my DMs. I froze for a moment when I saw it was from him. Fake Heath Hall. He'd actually responded, and I found I was nervous to see what he'd said. No, this selfish fake spy hero wasn't going to make me nervous. I clicked on the icon.

Well, I usually don't do repeats, but now that I know it bothered you so much, I might take another run at the pool.

My mouth dropped open.

"What did he say?" Amelia asked, leaning close to look.

I tilted my phone toward her and she let out a gasp. "Do you think he means it?"

I grunted. "Yes."

"You told him you were going to expose him?" she asked, obviously reading the message I had sent him. "But you don't know who he is."

"I was bluffing. He called me on it."

"He totally did." She laughed.

I returned my phone to the table. "It is now my goal to find out."

"Find out . . . ?"

"Who he is."

"Uh-oh," she said. "He's in trouble. You always accomplish your goals."

"Exactly," I said.

Amelia smiled, then her attention was drawn across the restaurant. "Now I'm starting to think that every guy could be fake Heath Hall. Like that guy in the booth over there. If I tilt my head and squint a little, he actually looks a little like Heath."

"So you think the guy under the mask actually looks like Heath Hall?"

"Yes. That's probably why he picked that particular

mask. People probably always tell him that he looks like Heath Hall and so he decided to capitalize on it."

I looked at the guy in the corner booth—squinted my eyes and tilted my head. He did look a little like Heath— minus the scar and technology, obviously.

"I'm going to go ask him if he's the fake Heath Hall." Amelia stood.

"Go for it," I said, knowing she wouldn't.

She sat back down. "You're right. It's probably not him. I've never even seen that guy at our school."

I laughed. "Let's get together tomorrow with our laptops. We'll figure out who he really is. It shouldn't be that hard."

FIVE

The next day on my way out the door to Amelia's, I stopped by my mom's office to say goodbye. I found her on the phone in the middle of a conversation.

"I realize the run is still eight months away, but the work starts well in advance and most of our sponsors have already committed. We have to get T-shirts designed, our website up and running for registration. It's a long process."

I stood in the doorway for a minute, hoping she'd just look up and I'd wave, then point at my cell phone, letting her know she could call me if she had any questions.

I even cleared my throat a few times, but she never glanced my way. Instead, she wrote in neat, even strokes in the notebook on the desk in front of her. I knew how long these phone calls could last.

Her office was a maze of clear plastic bins, her preferred method of organization. I had no idea how she found anything. Each was stacked full of T-shirts or flyers or personalized pens or visors or who knew what else.

I noticed her cell phone sitting on the desk next to her so I sent a text: **Mom, I'm going to Amelia's.**

Her phone dinged and she looked at it, then up at me with an eye roll. I just smiled. She held up a finger to me.

Into her office phone she said, "I'll send you the paperwork, then, and get back to you next week. How does that sound?" After a pause she clicked her pen and set it on the desk with a nod. "Okay. Thank you so much."

She ended the call, then set down the phone.

I nodded toward it. "You didn't even give yourself a two-week break? Already working on the next event?"

"Fund-raising breaks for no one."

"How is it going? Getting sponsors?"

"We're on track." She glanced at her watch, then looked up. "Isn't this early for you and Amelia?"

"I wouldn't exactly call ten a.m. 'early.'"

She smiled. "You know what I mean."

"We have a project we're working on," I said. She

probably thought I meant something for school, but it was easier to let her think that than explain what we were really up to. "Can I take the car?"

"Sure. What time will you be home?"

"I'm not sure. Can I text you?"

"Sounds good. See you later."

I nodded, thought about weaving through her plastic bin maze to give her a hug but changed my mind when she picked up her phone again. As if she'd read my mind, she kissed the air in my general direction. I turned and headed toward the front door.

I nearly ran over my dad, who was on his way into the kitchen.

"Where are you off to?" he asked.

"Amelia's. I told Mom."

"Sounds good. Don't do anything stupid and remember who you are." This was his standard line when I was going anywhere.

"Yeah, yeah. I'll remember exactly who I am when I'm doing something stupid."

"Ha-ha." He playfully squeezed my arm, then looked over my shoulder down the hall. "Your mom still trying to swindle people out of their money?"

"Fund-raising breaks for no one."

He lowered his brow. "I'm pretty sure it breaks for me."

"Yeah, me too." I sighed. "Maybe she can let someone else be in charge of the next race."

"Are you going to suggest that to her or am I?"

"Totally your job. I'm too young to die." The second the words were out of my mouth I wished I could take them back. "Sorry."

He pulled me into a hug. "Don't be. You are. *Far* too young."

Two hours later, I sat on Amelia's bed, my laptop open in front of me, studying fake Heath Hall's account. I was writing down anyone who'd commented on his posts and especially those he'd commented back to. Amelia had her laptop open as well and she was furiously scribbling names into a notebook of the people from our school who followed him. He had about six hundred followers, so it was taking her a while to weed out the ones that went to our school.

"So thinking back to that night at the pool," Amelia said, pausing for a moment. "You can't remember *anything* about him?"

"I remembered *he* was a he," I said.

"Right." She tapped the notebook with the pen. "What about his ethnicity? Was he white? Black? Latino?"

"He was wearing a rash guard. And the light from the pool makes *everyone* all glowy."

She lowered her chin. "Seriously?"

"I was angry! And I was in my prerace zone! And . . . I don't know. I *think* he was white?"

"You are no help whatsoever." She picked up the notebook and ran her pen along the page, her lips moving silently as she did. "One hundred and seven people from our school follow him. If we weed out all the girls . . ." She counted again. "That's seventy-two. He must be one of these seventy-two."

I hugged one of her pillows to my chest. "You think the real person behind the mask follows his own fake profile?"

"Yes. I do. And do you know who is on this list of guys from our school who follow him?" She gave me a sympathetic look that I didn't understand.

"I have no idea," I said when I realized she was waiting for a response. "The fake Wolverine?"

"No. Robert."

I held back a gasp and managed to keep my expression in check.

"Robert," she said again as if I hadn't heard her loud and clear the first time. "As in, your ex."

"Yes. I got it," I said before she could say his name for a third time. I didn't want to think of my ex. I'd done a pretty good job of just that for the last several weeks. I didn't want to think about his smile or the way he rambled when he was nervous and sang off key when he wanted to make me laugh. The way he'd dumped me out of the blue for a really stupid reason.

"If Robert is following him, maybe he knows something." She waved her hand at my paper. "Did he comment on any of his posts?"

"No," I said curtly.

"You have to talk to him."

"What? No!" To be fair, Amelia wasn't a bad friend for suggesting I talk to the guy who had ripped out my heart. I just hadn't been completely honest with her about how "mutual" the breakup was. In reality, there was nothing mutual about it. Robert had broken up with me because he said I was too intense, too single-minded. So I took swimming seriously. It was my ticket to a good college. I had to.

"Come on. He'll tell you. Just ask."

I did not want to talk to Robert. I was over him . . . mostly. Talking to him would lead to a major relapse. I was sure of it. But maybe she was right. Maybe he really would know who this guy was. Why else would he follow a fake account? It didn't seem like him at all. So he obviously had some sort of vested interest in what was happening. At the very least, he'd probably been to a few of the other disturbances caused by the guy. Maybe he'd seen something.

My eyes drifted to the wall above Amelia's bed, where a painting of a distorted fish hung. I had always liked the painting: it reminded me of how it felt sometimes being under the water—a separate body experience. Amelia said her brother's girlfriend, Abby, had painted it. Her brother was a few years older than her. Sometimes when I saw them together I tried to picture if my brother and I would've had a similar relationship—both loving and annoying at the same time. The way my parents described him, it seemed like we would've been close.

A knock sounded on the door, then Cooper poked his head in. "Amelia, Mom wants to know if you want lunch." Cooper's eyes lit up when he saw me. "Oh, hey, Hadley. I didn't know you were here."

"Yes, hi." I blushed a little. Cooper was cute, and for some reason, I felt like the fact that I had just been thinking about him was written all over my face.

"Tell Mom we'll be there in a minute," Amelia said.

"Will do." He shut the door.

Amelia's attention was back on me. "So? What do you think?"

"I wasn't thinking about anything."

She furrowed her brow. "Gross, I don't want to know. I was referring to Robert. Will you talk to him?"

"Oh. Yes. I will," I said, glad for the chance to move past my embarrassing thought process.

"I'll go with you," she said, maybe realizing it would be hard for me.

"Okay." I took the notebook from her and scanned the list. "Seventy-two," I said. "We'll talk to Robert first, but if he doesn't know anything, we need to work our way down this list. Someone has to know something. Right?"

"Agreed," she said with a nod.

My stomach twisted in a knot. I had to talk to Robert. The guy I'd been avoiding for the last month. This would not be fun.

SIX

My heart fluttered at the sight of Robert. So I had been right to avoid him for the last month, but it obviously wasn't long enough—there were still feelings lingering under the surface that I needed to stomp out for good. His blond hair seemed longer than I remembered, and his shoulders broader. His skin glowed with a tan from all his time running or at the beach. He liked the beach. I had successfully not thought about that and many other things about him and here we were heading straight for his car in the parking lot. I wanted to turn around and leave, but right as I stopped to do so, he looked up and met my eyes. If I left now, he'd know he still had an effect on me. He would not have an effect on me.

Amelia gave an excited bounce next to me. I self-consciously smoothed back my hair. Why had we decided to find him right after swim practice? He had track after school, so I figured there would be less people around, but I hadn't thought about how I'd look. A piece of wet hair stuck to my temple. I tucked it behind my ear, feeling heat creep up my cheeks. It wasn't like Robert hadn't seen me like this before. But still, here he was after a month, looking amazing. I wanted to look amazing too. Or at least a couple steps up from awful.

"Hey, Robert," Amelia said.

He gave my body a quick look up and down, as if checking to see if he had made the right decision. He must've decided he had because he didn't even smile. "Hi, Amelia. Hadley."

"So we were online the other day and noticed you follow Heath Hall," Amelia spit out.

Wow. No buildup at all. Just straight to the topic. I widened my eyes at her. She just smiled. She totally got away with stuff like that because she was so cute, even with her wet hair and swim sweats.

Robert laughed. "He's not the real one."

I furrowed my brow. "There is no real one. He's a movie character."

Amelia elbowed me. "We were just wondering if you knew who he really was," she said.

Robert met my eyes then and held my stare for a three count, my cheeks completing their transformation to red, before Amelia interrupted by asking again, "So? Do you know him?"

"Yes . . . sort of. He goes here."

"That's what we'd heard."

"Who is he?" I asked.

"I can't tell you. You have to figure that out on your own."

"Figure it out?" I asked.

"Yes." But that's all he said.

I wondered if he would've told Amelia had she asked the question, if he was holding back the info because it was me who wanted to know. It wasn't the best breakup. Even though he was the breaker-upper, it had been obvious that night that he thought I'd tell him that he was more important than swimming. That I'd beg him not to go, promise not to practice as much or that I'd spend more time with him or something. But I hadn't. Because it wasn't true. "Why is his identity some secret?"

A loud voice called from across the parking lot, "Robert!"

He whirled toward the sound, then let out a yodel. And without even a backward glance at us to say goodbye, he bounded over to his friend and they bumped chests.

I took in a deep breath and willed my body to return to its normal state.

Amelia ran the toe of her shoe along a crack in the asphalt and then, as if it was the one withholding information from us, looked up with a scowl. "That was useless. He only told us information we already knew." She studied my face. "Your cheeks are red."

I tugged at the neck of my hoodie. "I'm hot."

She squinted her eyes and focused on something over my shoulder, probably Robert. Then her eyes lit up. "Do you still like Robert? Is that why you're so flustered?"

"Can we walk away from his car before he comes back?"

"Of course." We headed for her car, the only one left in the back row of the parking lot. "So tell me, what's going on? If you still like him, I can come up with another good excuse to talk to him. Should I ask if he wants to go get hot wings with us?"

"Hot wings?"

"I'm hungry. Can we go get something to eat? I'll ask him if he wants to eat with us."

I grabbed her arm before she could go through with this plan. "He broke up with me. It wasn't mutual. He said I had a one-track mind."

"What? Hadley! Why didn't you tell me?"

"Shh." I could hear Robert's voice behind us still. I was sure he could hear us.

Amelia lowered her voice. "Sorry. But you should've told me. We could've bad-mouthed him together all these weeks."

"I just wanted to forget about it. I felt stupid. I had liked him." I obviously still did. But nothing had changed. If he didn't like what was important to me, or at least understand why it was important, there was no chance for us.

"*He* should feel stupid. You're amazing. Don't let his blindness make you feel bad about yourself. You have a passion and you work hard at it." She made a weird noise in the back of her throat that I recognized immediately as a noise Robert made. "So annoying."

I laughed.

"Of course you're too focused for him because he is a lazy pig."

I smiled. "He's not lazy. He's on the track team."

"Shhhh," she said. "We're venting."

We reached her car and I dug out of my backpack the notebook we had been using the day before. I drew a line through Robert. "Okay, seventy-one more people to go."

She started the car. "What do you think Robert meant by 'figure that out on your own'?"

"I don't know." We both watched as his car backed

out of the space and drove through the parking lot, like it would somehow answer our question. It didn't . . . obviously. She took the list from me, ran her finger down the page and then ripped it in half. "Well, we're going to figure it out together. We'll divide and conquer."

I took a deep breath and shoved my half of the list back into my backpack.

The next day, I stared at the names on my *Who Is Heath Hall?* list. I didn't have to do this. What were the odds that he'd show up at my swim meet again this Friday? The image of him jumping into the pool made my shoulders go tense immediately. I growled. Apparently, I *did* need to do this.

I scanned the list. I'd start with the people I semi-knew, like Brady Thompson. Then I'd move on to the total strangers. Brady sat two seats to the left of me in math.

Five minutes before class ended, I packed my book away and readied myself to cut him off on his way out the door. I felt like I was planning some sort of attack. I wiped my hands on my jeans. The bell rang right in the middle of Mr. Kingston telling us our homework assignment. I stood, my movement making the chair scrape the floor.

"I haven't dismissed you yet," Mr. Kingston said.

I sat back down. He held us an extra minute, then finally let us leave. I caught up to Brady at the door and followed him several steps out of it before I said, "Brady, hi. Um . . ."

He looked around, then right at me. "Hadley Moore. Are you talking to me?" If it weren't for the smile on his face, I might've thought he was being rude.

Even with the smile, I hesitated. "Yes. Can I ask you a quick question?"

"If I can ask you one?"

"Okay."

"Where is your music today?" He pointed to my ears that were free of the headphones I normally wore between classes.

I patted my pocket where they were stashed.

"I see. Okay, go ahead."

I cleared my throat. "I noticed that you follow Heath Hall online."

"Not the real one."

Was everyone going to point that out? "I know. But I was wondering if you know who he really is. Like, who wears the mask? He goes to our school, right?"

He laughed at this like he thought I was making some inside joke with him.

I waited until he was done to say, "So you don't know who he is?"

"If you don't, I'm not going to be the one to tell you."

I curled my lip. Was this some kind of pact? First Robert, now Brady.

"I knew it wouldn't last long," he said.

"What?" I gave him a sideways glance.

He pointed at my hand that was clutching an earbud and getting ready to put it in my ear. "I guess we're done."

"Oh. Right. Thanks." I pushed Play with my opposite hand and let the music drown out my thoughts.

"Do people think I'm a jerk?" I asked Amelia when I joined her at our usual table in the middle of the outdoor courtyard for lunch.

"Someone called you a jerk? Who?" She put her hands on the metal table like she was ready to stand up and fight whomever I named.

"No. Nobody did. Just something Brady said today."

"Brady Thompson? What did he say?" She moved her hands to under her chin, then let out a dreamy sigh. "And how did he say it?"

I smiled and opened my bag of carrot sticks. "He was surprised I was talking to him. Acted like I never had before."

"Have you?"

"Well, not outside of class or anything . . . but that's not the point. I don't purposefully ignore him. I'm not rude or anything. Am I?"

"No . . . You just have your music on most of the time and walk down the hall like you know exactly where you're going."

"I *do* know exactly where I'm going. Doesn't everybody?"

She pointed a potato chip at me. "But other people take their time getting there. You know, by talking to other students like they actually like them."

"I like people." I circled a carrot stick in the air. "I did that whole swim race thing with Jackson."

"That had nothing to do with liking him and everything to do with the fact that you lost your race that night and you needed to win at something."

I narrowed my eyes and bit into my carrot. "Fine, you're right. But Robert! What about him? I dated him. And Miguel before him."

"True. They were both confident enough to date someone as independent as you. Well, until Robert wasn't, apparently. Have I mentioned yet today how stupid he is?"

I smiled, but these arguments weren't proving my case at all. "DJ!" I exclaimed. "I talk to DJ."

"Because you know he is unavailable."

"So you're saying that Brady is right? That people think I'm closed off?"

She sighed. "No. I mean, sort of. You're just private. You like to keep most things to yourself. But you can be friendly, nice, when you want to be. We're best friends, after all."

Exactly. We were best friends. . . . Granted, I'd known her since second grade. I wondered if she would've given me a chance if we had met now, in high school. She was much more open than I was. Willing to let people in. Willing to give people the chance to have control over her emotions. It took a lot of trust for me to get there.

"You're like the big swim star at the school, Hadley," Amelia added. "You can be intimidating."

"I am not intimidating."

"You are. I thought that's what you were counting on when you finally get to confront the masked man."

"You're right, it is." She was right, why was I getting hung up on this? I liked my life. I liked my emotions safe. Who cared what Brady or anyone else thought, for that matter? They had no idea how I really was.

I glanced around the courtyard. "So were you able to check anyone off your list?"

She shook her head. "They aren't talking. They won't give him up. It's frustrating. I even talked to some girls not on our list. A few said they've seen his posts but couldn't care less who he is. One person swore it was Thomas Freeman and another said it was Liam Baker."

I raised my eyebrows. "Did you add them to the list?"

"I did."

"You talked to a lot of people," I said.

"How many have you talked to?"

"Just the one."

She bit her lip, pulled out a pen, and crossed off several people. "I really only talked to three from our list and then added the two, so I'm only one down too."

"We need to figure this out before Friday."

"What's Friday?" she asked.

"Our next swim meet."

She pursed her lips. "We studied his pattern online yesterday and he usually doesn't show up to the same place twice."

"Until I taunted him, apparently. I can't risk it. I have a winning record to maintain. Heath Hall will not ruin that."

SEVEN

Dylan Sutter was next on my list. And as I left the science building and headed through the outdoor halls toward the pool, I saw him wrestling with a book at his locker. I stepped up beside him into the shade structure that covered the rows of lockers. "Dylan."

His book fell to the ground with a slap. He started to retrieve it when he met my eyes with a stunned expression before dropping his gaze to my shoulder.

"I noticed that you follow Heath Hall online. I know he's not the actual actor who plays him," I added before he had the chance to inform me of that.

"Yeah." He went back to trying to fit his book in his too-full locker.

"So who is he?"

"You don't know?"

Obviously, I wanted to say but instead just said, "No."

He shook his head back and forth several times, then slammed his locker, his hand barely making it out. He pushed on the door once more as though he thought the books inside were about to shove it back open. Satisfied, he straightened up, then glared at my shoulder. "Can't tell if you don't know."

Holy crap, how did this guy get all these people to keep their mouths shut? This was turning out to be way more work than I had anticipated. "Dylan. Look. I won't tell anyone. I just need to talk to him."

"You can't just talk to him. Well, I mean you can but you can't."

What? "What is he, the Godfather? Come on."

Dylan adjusted his backpack on his shoulder and stumbled a little under the weight of it. "Can't tell you if you don't know," he said again, then nodded his head at the ground and left.

I smacked Dylan's locker as if it was the one that had refused to spill its secrets and I turned to leave, walking straight into Jackson. "Moore, I should've known it was you."

I took a step back. "What?"

"What did you say to Dylan?"

"What?" Why did I keep saying that?

"Dylan." He pointed behind him, where I watched Dylan glance over his shoulder once, see us looking, then nearly trip over his own feet before righting himself and continuing forward.

"I said nothing."

"It didn't look like nothing."

"Are you spying on me?" I asked.

"I was walking down the hall. So yes, I guess that means I was spying. I thought maybe I could learn your secret swimming powers for the next time someone strands me on an island in the middle of a lake."

"Strands you? That's a little dramatic, don't you think? If you weren't a strong swimmer, you shouldn't have swum out there."

"I'm a strong swimmer. I did beat you, after all."

I started to protest, to tell him he only beat me because he cheated, but I stopped myself. That's what he wanted me to do.

He bent down and picked up something off the ground by my foot. When he stood, I noticed it was my earbuds. I held out my hand for them. "Oh, thanks."

He just tucked them into his pocket. "I better go turn these in to Lost and Found."

"They're mine." I kept my palm outstretched.

"They were just sitting on the cement. They could be anyone's."

I sighed. "Jackson. They're mine."

He took them out of his pocket and held them over my hand. When I reached for them, he tugged them just out of my grasp. He laughed and did the exact same thing again. "You just have to grab them."

"Why are you such a child?" Even his hair seemed to laugh at life. It was a curly mop on top of his head that he didn't feel the need to tame.

"Why are you always so serious?" He dropped them onto my hand.

I wasn't serious all the time. I had fun around the right people. Just not people who thought life was a big joke.

As if reading my mind, the smile on Jackson's face disappeared. "Hey," he said in a tone as sincere as his new expression. "I'm sorry if I offended you the other day. I didn't think my joke out in the lake would scare you."

"I . . ." wasn't sure how to finish that sentence. I was sure he was seconds away from laughing and saying, *Just kidding.*

"You . . . ?" he prompted.

"Yeah. No big deal. It didn't really scare me."

"I think what you meant to say was, 'Jack, not only did you not scare me, I thought it was hilarious. You're the funniest person I know.'"

A breeze filled with salty ocean air blew a piece of my hair across my face. I pushed it out of the way. "Why is it so important that I find you funny? The rest of the school feeds your ego enough."

"You're the last holdout."

"I'm positive I'm not the last."

"Really? Have you started a club?"

I smiled a little. "Maybe I should. The Jack-haters club."

"I'd totally join that club."

I shook my head. "I bet you would."

He gave my arm a playful punch. "See you around."

At home I opened my computer, ready to look for more clues. Surely Heath Hall had to have said something to give himself away at some point. Right away I zeroed in on his latest post. *Heath Hall: I'll be at the museum on Tenth Street this Thursday sometime between the hours of 7 and 10.*

He'd given another location.

I pulled out my cell and dialed Amelia's number.

She answered the phone with the words, "I saw. That's Abby's museum. They have a show this week. Do you think he's trying to ruin it?"

"I don't know if he's *trying* to, but that always seems to be the end result. So are we going?" I asked.

"Of course."

"Ms. Lin would be so proud," I said. Ms. Lin was the art teacher at school. I had never taken art, but she was my mentor teacher and was constantly trying to get me to change this fact.

"I know. That's why we shouldn't tell her. She'll think we've decided to become artists after all."

"She thinks everyone's an artist waiting to find themselves," I said.

"So do you think I should warn Abby?" Amelia said. "Or my brother?"

"Yes, you should let them know there might be a disruption at the museum." If someone had warned me, it might not have affected me so much.

"You know, Heath Hall busted that museum heist and saved the priceless painting in movie number three."

"Um . . . so? You know this guy isn't really Heath Hall. As we've been told a million times."

"Maybe it's a clue, though. Maybe he plans where to go based on the plots of the movies."

"Has there been a movie that involved swimming?" I asked, searching my memory for that answer.

"He's constantly swimming. Usually scuba diving to break into some fancy building," Amelia said.

"But what does that have to do with the school pool?"

"Who knows? Maybe we'll figure it out Thursday at

seven. You and me at the museum."

"For sure. Is this a dress-up kind of event?" I rarely wore dresses except once or twice a year for charity events my parents made me go to. My mom had picked out every single one of those dresses so I wasn't even sure if I had anything that would work for this.

"Yes. I'll find you a dress."

Before I had a chance to say anything else, my door swung open. My mom stood in it holding up two T-shirts. "Which one do you like better?" she asked.

"Amelia, I'll talk to you later."

"Okay."

"Oh, sorry, I didn't know you were on the phone," Mom said after I hung up.

"It's okay." I looked at the two shirts she held. They were both light blue. One had tennis shoes running across the top of the words *Five K*. The other had a ribbon tying *Five* and *K* together.

"They're both bad, aren't they?" she said, scrutinizing them. "I should tell the designer to try something else."

"No, Mom. They're fine. I like the tennis shoes one."

"Tennis shoes?"

I pointed to the one on the right.

"Those aren't tennis shoes. Great. They're supposed to be beakers."

"Beakers? Why would you have beakers on a shirt

about running a five K?"

"To show that the money raised will go to science to help find a cure."

I turned my head sideways, trying to see as beakers what clearly looked like tennis shoes to me. I couldn't. "Oh. Okay. Well, that works too."

"Back to the drawing board," she said, draping the shirts over one shoulder and leaving my room.

"Try tennis shoes!" I yelled after her.

"I love you!" she yelled back.

My attention was drawn back to my computer, still open in front of me, a picture of Heath Hall filling my screen. "What is your story?" I stretched my hands above my head to loosen up my shoulders—they felt much better today.

It was only Tuesday. Thursday and the museum seemed forever away. If we could figure out who Heath Hall was before that, then maybe I wouldn't have to put on an Amelia-chosen dress.

EIGHT

Coach was standing over my lane when I finished my laps. He looked at his watch. Had he been timing me? I pulled off my goggles and earphones.

"Moore. Everyone else is gone."

I looked at the lanes on either side of me. Sure enough, they were empty.

"If you can't hear the end whistle, maybe you should stop listening to music while you swim."

"You know, most coaches are happy that their athletes want to swim longer than they have to. You should be glad for my dedication and perseverance."

He cracked a smile. "Really? How many coaches are you basing this opinion on?"

"Just you."

"That's what I thought."

"And most coaches would want to reward me for my hard work by allowing me to swim the butterfly this Friday."

He ran his hand over his hair a few times. "I've told you this before. It's too close to the freestyle. I need you strong for that one. Now get out of my pool so I can go home and see my family."

I pushed myself out of the pool, wincing a little at the slight pain in my right shoulder. It wasn't too bad today, though.

"And I'm serious about ditching the crutch," he called after me.

I gripped my headphones tighter. They weren't a crutch; they helped me concentrate.

As I headed toward the locker room, the sky already on fire with the setting sun, I saw Robert standing by the gate, leaning against one of the posts. My stomach fluttered. I hesitated, not sure if he was waiting to talk to me or not. I hadn't seen him at the pool since we'd broken up. Before, I would've given him a big hug, soaking the front of his shirt and he would've pretended to be mad about it. But today his arms were crossed in front of his chest, not exactly a welcoming pose. He had on sunglasses, even though they were past necessary, so I couldn't tell if he was even looking at me. If he wanted to talk to me, he'd need to say so. I picked up my towel and wrapped it around me.

"Hadley," he said when I was closer.

I turned toward him, keeping a good twenty feet between us. "Yeah?"

He didn't move either, just leaned there against the metal post of the chain-link fence. "You still have some of my things. Could you bring them to school tomorrow?"

"Some of your things? Like what?"

"Like my Nike sweatshirt."

I slept in that sweatshirt at least once a week . . . maybe more. "What Nike sweatshirt?"

"The navy one with the red lettering."

"Okay, I'll bring it tomorrow." I loved that sweatshirt but it was time I let it go. Let him all the way go. "Anything else?"

"I think I left my math book there too."

"How have you been doing your math homework?"

"Borrowing from Tony."

I hadn't seen his math book. "I'll look for it."

"Okay." He finally straightened up from his lean but didn't move to leave. "Thanks."

"Sure." I needed to be the one to leave first. He had been the first last time, after all. I surprised myself by actually acting on that thought.

"Hadley." He stopped me before I got too far. "Did you find out about Heath Hall?"

That question had me turning back around. "Not yet. Did you want to tell me who he is?"

"No. He's going to be at the museum tomorrow, though."

I leveled him with an annoyed stare. Really? He still wasn't going to tell me, but he was trying to make sure I remembered he knew? Those few butterflies left in my stomach were going to be easier to crush than I'd thought. "I saw that online."

He shifted from one foot to the other. "So . . . you're going?"

I looked at his feet, which were still shifting his weight back and forth. Why was he nervous? "You're surprised?"

"You're not exactly an art fan. Plus, it doesn't seem like something you'd do."

"Maybe you don't know me very well." Why had he shown up here at swim practice, bringing all his memories with him and claiming to know my habits? "You could've just texted me, you know."

"What?"

"About the sweatshirt and math book."

He pointed toward the track field across the parking lot. "I was here. Knew you would be too."

Of course he knew that. It's why we broke up, after all. I was too single-minded. Is that why he didn't think I'd go to the museum?

He shoved his hands in the pockets of his shorts, his head lowering a bit, all his bravado gone. Why did this version have to show up?

"It's just, why are you getting caught up in the Heath Hall thing? I figured you'd mock him and write him off."

He was right, that was exactly what I would've done . . . had been doing since I first heard about Heath Hall. There was no way I was going to tell him that the *only* reason I was now interested was because I was trying to protect my swimming. If he knew that, it would only prove everything he ever thought about me. I set my jaw. Then something he said occurred to me. "What do you mean, you 'figured I'd write him off'? Did you have something to do with him showing up at the swim meet?"

Did he send him there to punish me? I wondered for a brief moment if Robert actually was Heath Hall. But just like he knew me well, I knew him, and although Robert liked attention, he would never show up at a public event claiming to be someone he wasn't for a bit of notoriety.

"What? No . . . never mind. Bring my stuff tomorrow." His indifferent face was back before he walked away. Again. I was supposed to walk away first this time.

I was grumbling when I entered the building that housed the locker rooms. Apparently, I wasn't paying attention either because I nearly plowed down DJ. He dropped a stack of papers that scattered upon impact with the floor.

"Sorry," I said.

He lowered himself to his knees and gathered them. I helped, my towel restricting my usefulness.

"It's okay. You're here late."

"So are you." Just as I was about to pick up one of the pages, I saw my name at the top. I reached for it to get a better look when DJ snatched it from beneath my fingers and stood, arms full of disorganized pages.

"What are those?"

"Just time sheets and stuff," he said, but I could tell that's not what they were.

"But it said, 'one hundred butterfly,' under my name. I've never raced in the butterfly." At least not since starting high school.

"You've swum it in practice."

DJ wasn't a very good liar. "Is Coach going to let me swim it on Friday? Is that what it's about?"

"No . . . I mean, I'm not sure. But that's not what these

are." He clutched the papers tighter as if I had X-ray vision and could see through them.

"What are they, then?"

"Hadley, stop. I know you think your persistence is charming, but it can be frustrating at times."

I gripped the top of my towel, glad to know every guy in the universe found my determination off-putting. My eyes stung with the insult.

"I'm sorry. That came out wrong. I didn't mean to hurt your feelings," he said.

"No. You didn't." I moved to walk around him and he stepped in front of me.

"Hadley. I'm sorry. You are every coach's dream. Persistence is key to what you do."

"DJ, don't worry about it. I'm fine. See you around."

"Hadley," he said, but I was already through the door to the girls' locker room, glad he couldn't follow me in there.

NINE

Amelia was late. It was 6:35. She was supposed to pick me up at 6:30. I sat at the counter in the kitchen, more dressed up than I'd been in a while. My hair was up in a bun, I wore the black dress that Amelia swore wasn't too tight, and I was even wearing heels. If she didn't get here soon, we were going to miss him. Tension had spread up from my shoulders and was beginning to settle in my neck.

I tapped the edge of my art show ticket on the counter several times. I checked my phone. It was 6:37 and there were no missed calls or texts from Amelia. I tried to call her again. She didn't answer. Ugh. Why didn't I have a car? Sometimes it sucked depending on others for transportation.

I knocked on my dad's bedroom door and opened it when he gave a muffled reply. "Hey, Dad. Can I borrow your truck?"

He was lying in bed reading a book, which he lowered to look at me. "I thought Amelia was picking you up."

"She's late."

He glanced at the clock on his nightstand. "Eight minutes late?"

"I need to be at the museum by seven."

"It's an open house–type thing. There's a three-hour window to see all the pieces. You probably won't need the whole three hours. Especially because I didn't think you enjoyed looking at art."

Why did everyone think I didn't appreciate art? Just because I wasn't artistic didn't mean I couldn't appreciate good art. But that wasn't the point. I needed the whole three hours to make sure I didn't miss Heath. If we missed him, we'd have to try something else, and so far, nothing else was working. We'd been talking to people all week and nobody knew anything concrete. I hoped Heath didn't wait until 9:55 to show up tonight because my feet were already killing me. "I know, it's just . . . we were meeting someone there at seven."

"I see. Yes, you can—"

A car horn from outside cut him off.

"Never mind! Thanks, Dad." I tripped my way out of his room, then steadied myself. I needed more practice walking in heels.

"Have fun," he called after me. "And remember who you are!"

"Already forgot!" I called back, then pulled the door shut behind me.

I hurried to Amelia's car. "Took you long enough," I said when I got inside.

"Sorry. My mom borrowed my shoes and didn't remember where she'd put them. I was trying to find them and Cooper thought it was the time to blockade me from going into each room."

"That's annoying."

"You are so lucky you don't have to deal with siblings." Right as she said it, she sucked in her lips. "Wow. I'm sorry. I'm a loser. You can hit me as hard as you want in the arm." She held out her arm like I was really going to do it.

I stared at Eric's truck, up there on its pedestal, as she pulled down the driveway and out onto the street. In a way she was right. I didn't have to deal with siblings. But in a way she was so very wrong. "No, it's okay. I knew what you meant. Did you end up warning Abby and your brother about tonight?" I asked.

"Yes. They both kind of blew it off. Abby said they have security at the museum, then added, 'We've met the real Heath Hall, so we won't be impressed.'"

"So she thinks he won't be able to get in?"

"Or something. Cooper just laughed and said he remembered a few things fake Heath Hall had done in their day, then patted my head."

"Their day? Like two years ago?"

"Yeah. I decided that maybe they deserve a little trouble tonight."

I laughed. "Speaking of trouble. I forgot to tell you what happened after practice the other night."

"You mean Robert showing up? I've been thinking about that. Do you think he's Heath Hall?"

"I thought about it for like a second, but no, I don't. I don't even think he likes Heath Hall movies." I shook my head. "But that's not what I meant. I was going to tell you about . . ." I stopped because Amelia had just pulled into the parking lot and I saw someone standing there in a suit. "DJ."

"I invited him," Amelia said.

"And he *came*?"

Amelia wiggled her eyebrows. "Apparently, he's not completely out of my league and doesn't have a problem with the whole dog-years thing."

"He is . . . I was going to tell you about *him*."

"About DJ?"

"Yes. This is going to be very awkward." I hadn't talked to him since our uncomfortable exchange outside the locker room.

She parked and turned off the car. "Why? DJ's great. So what happened?"

"I'll have to explain later," I said because DJ opened her door. I swallowed down the hurt I still felt over what he'd said to me yesterday and I pulled my door open. I didn't have a problem pretending things were fine. I'd had lots of practice.

"Hey, Hadley," DJ said with a small smile, like he was still trying to apologize. "Amelia said the whole swim team was coming tonight but you two are the first I've seen."

I raised my eyebrows at Amelia. "Doesn't have a problem with dog years?"

She waved her hand at me, then said to DJ, "I said the whole swim team *might* come tonight. I guess I was wrong."

Amelia bounced up and down as we walked toward the entrance. "I'm so excited for the museum tonight."

"I didn't realize you had such an appreciation of art,"

DJ said, clearly oblivious to what our true mission was.

"We do," I assured him. "Very much so."

"How do you say art in Spanish?" Amelia asked.

"La arte. El artes. It all depends on how you use it in a sentence."

There were a few people waiting to get in at the entrance ahead of us. The sound of the waves crashing just beyond the building reminded me that it had been a while since I'd been to the beach.

"If I push my way through them, will we get kicked out?" Amelia whispered.

An older woman looked over her shoulder at us and we both stifled laughs. When we finally made it inside, we all stopped in the entrance. Huge jellyfish hung from the ceiling three stories up, their tentacles dangling nearly to our level.

"Is it an underwater theme?" Amelia asked.

I looked at my ticket. "It doesn't say."

As we stood in the lobby, looking up at the three floors above us, I felt like I was in a fishbowl. Not just because of the circular shape of the museum and pale blue walls but because people on each floor stood at the gleaming silver railings, staring down.

"Where should we start?" I asked.

"Let's find Abby. She'll tell us if she's seen anything interesting yet."

We found her on the second floor by a huge piece made of paper. She wore a cute knee-length dress and a blue blazer. She smiled when she saw us. "Well, hello. It's my conspiracy theorists."

"I take it nothing out of the ordinary has happened?" Amelia asked her.

"Not yet, but we're just getting started," she said. "We have time."

"Exactly," Amelia answered.

"Is there a program that shows the artists on display tonight? This is a local art show, right?" I asked.

"It is. And yes, did you not get a program at the door?" She handed me a trifold, shiny white program. I looked through it as DJ and Amelia studied some paintings down the hall. Was Amelia losing interest in the Heath Hall investigation?

The program was completely unhelpful. There were names next to each and every piece, none of which I recognized. I sighed. "You don't have any pieces in the show tonight?"

"Not this time. I'm gearing up for a summer art program I'm doing."

"That's cool."

"It should be."

"Well, I'm going to look around."

"Yes, enjoy," Abby said.

I found Amelia and DJ on opposite sides of a large fish statue. Their heads were angled to the side. "What are you guys doing?"

"It says to find the hidden shapes in its scales," DJ said.

I stared at the fish for a moment, then found myself tilting my head. Maybe I *didn't* appreciate art because I didn't get it at all. I rolled the program in my hands and turned a circle. That's when I saw Brady across the way heading up some stairs. I elbowed Amelia's side and nodded toward him.

"You think he knows where this thing is going down tonight?" she whispered.

"I think that's our best bet." Our only bet at this point. DJ wandered a bit, leaving us by the fish. "And, seriously, DJ is kind of cramping our style. How are we supposed to investigate with him here?"

"I hadn't thought about that before now."

"Obviously."

"His cuteness blinded me to logistics. Let's send him on an impossible quest."

"Like what?"

"Leave it to me." She approached DJ. "I heard there was this art piece here tonight that I'm dying to see. I don't remember the artist's name but it's of a boy looking at the ocean. We're going to check the third floor. Will you look around this one?"

"Of course."

"Okay, we'll meet up again in a little bit."

He walked away and we went for the stairs. By the time we reached them, Brady was gone but someone else was climbing them.

"Isn't that Dylan Sutter?" Amelia asked as we headed up.

"Is it?" I shuffled us sideways so we could get a better look. Dylan was using the handrail and walking slowly up each step, almost as if he had to make the decision to continue up for each and every stair he took. "It totally is. Do you think he's . . . ?"

From behind us a voice said, "Hadley Moore. I didn't expect to see you here tonight. And without your earphones."

We turned to see Jackson Holt.

TEN

"Maybe Jackson is Heath," Amelia whispered.

I considered that thought for a moment. It wouldn't surprise me. "Jackson? What are you doing here?"

"I think I'm here for the same reason you are."

"Heath Hall?"

He nodded, which meant he wasn't Heath Hall . . . right? He held his elbows out, one for each of us. "Shall we?"

Amelia immediately let go of me and latched onto him. I kept my hands to myself but walked next to him as we all continued up the stairs.

"I'm Amelia, by the way," she said.

"Oh, right." I realized it was my job to introduce them. I'd thought they knew each other. "Jackson, Amelia. Amelia, Jackson."

"We've met at school before, right?" he said.

"I've seen you around," she said. "Last time was in the lake behind Sarah's house, challenging my best friend to a competition you knew she couldn't refuse."

"Did I win that competition?" he asked with a half smile. "I don't remember."

I grunted.

Three flights of stairs in heels wasn't easy, and Jackson's company wasn't helping. I would find the elevator for the way down for sure.

When we finally made it upstairs, everyone was filing into a room called the Diamond Room. Jackson went in ahead of us. I grabbed hold of Amelia's arm so she wouldn't join up with him again, and we stepped inside. At the far end of the room several people were moving a giant painting into place as though they'd just brought it in. It wasn't labeled like the others in the museum had been but it was amazing. Reds and blues and purples created an abstract ocean. Tossed in the waves was a ship that was falling apart, wooden pieces strewn in the water around it. Goose bumps appeared along my arms. Now *that* was art.

"Is that painting his?" Amelia asked. "Heath Hall's?"

"Fake Heath Hall," I said under my breath. "You think that painting has something to do with his post?"

"I don't know but are all these people here to support him?"

"What?" I looked around the room and realized it was full of people from our school. "I guess they saw his post just like we did."

"True."

"Split up?" I asked. I recognized so many people from the list we'd made and now they were all here in the same place. This would save me so much time.

She nodded, and we headed in opposite directions.

I wasn't sure who to talk to first. Was one of these people about to whip out a mask and run around the museum? Or were they really all here just because they'd seen the post like we had?

I saw Brady again, and even though I'd already talked to him at school, he had confessed to knowing something. Maybe he'd be more likely to share if he thought I was in the know now. I joined him. "He should be here any minute," I said.

"Yep," Brady answered back. He was staring at the large canvas that leaned against the far wall, its movers gone. "I don't believe he was worried about this," Brady mumbled. "Misuse."

"What do you mean?" I asked.

"Nothing."

Just when I was about to move on to talk to someone else, the lights went out. Then a single spotlight from someone's phone lit up the large painting. Another phone shined on a guy dressed in a tux making his way through the crowd. I couldn't see where Amelia had gone or if she had been anywhere near where this guy materialized. He walked until he stood in front of the large painting, back to us. So here he was, the guy who'd ruined my race.

"I think that's Brad McCall," I heard someone whisper behind me.

"Maybe but I heard Heath was Leo Morales."

Both those names were on our list.

Up front, Heath Hall stared at the painting for a long time. Someone to my right gave a supportive holler and then several others joined in. Soon the room began to clap and cheer. At last, the guy in front of the painting turned around and bowed. He was wearing the mask.

His posture was slouched, his hands in the pockets of his tux. When he spoke, his voice was muffled, like he was distorting it on purpose. I had to strain to hear because it was also quiet.

"Thanks everyone for the support. Showing my work has been a fear of mine for a long time. And the reactions I've gotten from you all on my piece tonight mean a lot to me." He lifted his hand in a wave and then stepped away from the painting.

"That's it?" I asked no one in particular.

"Yep," Brady answered. "That's it. Until next time."

I couldn't wait that long. My eyes hadn't left him since he stepped away from that painting. My vision had adjusted somewhat to the dark and I watched him head for a back exit. I slid off my shoes, gripping the straps in my hand and ran after him.

The door closed just as I reached it and I pushed my way through. We were now in a back hallway, some sort of service area, nobody but the two of us. This was probably how he'd brought the unsanctioned painting into the museum. Heath was at the end of the corridor, about to round the corner. "Wait," I said.

He stopped. "You're not supposed to follow me."

"Who are you?"

He turned but looked ready to bolt, so I stayed where I was, not wanting to spook him. His hands were shaking so much that I could see them moving even though forty feet separated us. I took him in from head to toe, trying to find some sort of clue. But his tux was generic and his shoes, standard dress shoes. He was even wearing gloves.

I took a slow step forward. "I liked your painting. It was amazing."

"Thank you." He glanced to the side, his escape route.

"I won't tell anyone who you are. I'll keep it to myself."

"That's not how it works."

"How what works?" I pointed back toward the door we had both come through. "They know who you are. How come I can't?"

He wouldn't meet my eyes.

"If you can't tell me who you are, at least promise me this."

He gave a small nod.

"Please stay away from the swim meets from now on."

He gave another nod, bigger this time, then he took off. I ran after him but by the time I rounded the corner he was gone. The hallway split into two and there was no trace of him. I clenched my fists in frustration, a jolt of pain radiating through my shoulder as I did. I cringed and massaged it away. Not bothering to put my shoes back on, I made my way back to Amelia.

She was typing furiously into her phone.

"What are you doing?"

"Recording who was here before I forget. There were so many people. I swear it was nearly my entire list. This is really going to help us narrow it down."

"Did you happen to see Brad McCall or Leo Morales?"

I asked, remembering the names that had been whispered behind me earlier.

"Yes, actually." She showed me her phone. "Already on my list. Why?"

I gave a frustrated sigh. "Nothing."

"Where'd you disappear to?"

"I went after him."

She stopped typing and looked up. "Did you catch him?"

"Sort of, but that stupid mask made it impossible to tell who he was."

"That stupid mask was pretty awesome. I haven't seen it in person before, only online. How do you even get a mask that realistic? That would cost a serious amount of money."

I had forgotten she hadn't seen the mask at the pool. "So our Heath Hall is rich?"

"Wouldn't it be funny if it was Grant James wearing a Heath Hall mask?"

"It's not."

She shoved her phone into her purse. "I know. I said, 'Wouldn't it be funny?' Work with me here."

I smiled. "Yes, it would be funny."

"Thank you." She widened her eyes. "So what happened?"

"He ran off. I have no idea who he is. He was as

skittish as a baby rabbit, though."

"That's a clue. Maybe one that will help us."

I sighed. "I accomplished my mission. I told him to stay away from the pool. I don't really need to know who he is anymore." This was becoming more trouble than it was worth.

"And you think he'll listen."

"I think you were right anyway," I said, gesturing to the art around us. "I don't think he likes to do repeat appearances."

Two security guards talking into walkie-talkies rushed by us, toward the painting.

"They're a little late," Amelia said.

"We should probably go find DJ and rescue him from the cruel mission you sent him on," I said.

"Yes. We should've just told DJ about the Heath Hall thing. After seeing so many people from school up here, he probably wouldn't have found it weird."

"Probably not."

It took us searching every floor before we found DJ on the first. His tie was loosened, his collar beneath it unbuttoned, as if he was done being dressed up for the night. When he saw us, he smiled. "Still haven't found it. Did you have better luck?"

"We had no luck," I said.

"I found something else I want to show you." Amelia took his hand. As she pulled him away, she looked back at me and mouthed, *Do you mind?*

I shook my head no. Amelia had been crushing on DJ forever. And it seemed like she was actually making a tiny bit of progress. I wasn't going to get in the way of that. I stared after them for a while. A strip of white hung down below the back of his suit jacket and it took me a moment to realize it was his shirt. It must've come untucked. DJ was a mess. Cute but a mess. I turned and went to look at some art. I *was* at a museum, after all.

ELEVEN

"I don't believe Coach isn't letting you swim all four races today. I thought that's what the paper you caught DJ with was implying."

The cold metal bench beneath my legs made me shiver. "Amelia. Are you trying to get in my head right before we swim?"

"Sorry. Sorry. I'll be quiet."

But it wasn't her. I was already in my head. Coach didn't want me to swim all four races and I couldn't stop thinking about how DJ said my persistence was frustrating. How Coach probably felt the same way. He didn't even want me to stay late at practices anymore. He'd never said anything when I'd stayed late before.

Up in the stands my dad called my name. He stood and waved when I looked. I waved back and noted my mom next to him talking on the phone. I really should've worn my headphones right up until I had to swim. Michael Phelps used to do that at the Olympics to stay in the zone or get pumped up or something. If *he'd* done it, it couldn't have been a crutch like Coach implied. I took a deep breath of chlorine-filled air, then stood. I jumped up and down a few times, then stretched out my shoulders. "Here we go," I said when the announcer called out our race.

Coach was beaming when he stood in front of us after the meet. "I'm so proud of all of you. We had an amazing meet today. Next Saturday is the finals. You are to stay all day to support the whole team no matter when you swim. After that, as your coach I require one more commitment from each of you. In two weeks there's the awards banquet. I expect you all there. I don't want to hear about other plans. This will be your one and only if you expect to swim on my team next year. This is as important to me as any meet has been the whole season. Understood?"

"Understood," we all echoed back to him.

"Okay. Go enjoy your Friday."

The other swimmers filed away. Amelia left too, knowing my habits. This would normally be the time, after performing so well in my races, where I would pester the coach about letting me swim more. Even though I was sure he wouldn't let me swim the butterfly for the final meet of the season, I still had my senior year ahead of me. I wanted all four races next year. But over the coach's shoulder I saw DJ, and between the two of them, and my throbbing shoulders, I couldn't do it. Coach obviously didn't want it to happen. I spun around and left.

Amelia, who hadn't made it far, tilted her head.

"What?" I asked.

"Nothing," she said. "It's nice that Heath Hall didn't show up today. Turns out you're intimidating, after all."

"I guess so." My dad stood off to the side, waiting for me. "I'm riding home with my parents. See you tonight."

She gave me a side hug. "Don't give up on the four races."

"What's the point?"

"The point is that you're amazing."

"Until I can shave off more time, I'm going to stop asking."

My dad opened his arms when I joined him.

"You don't want a hug. I'm wet."

He pulled me into one anyway. "I always want a hug. You swam great today."

"Thanks, Dad."

"Mom said to tell you, 'Good job.'"

I wondered if she had seen me swim at all. Every time I had looked up, she was on her phone. My eyes went to the gate and to the parking lot beyond it, wondering if she was still on the phone now. I rubbed at my aching shoulders. "Where is she?"

"She had to run off to her first five K meeting today with the new staff for the next race."

"Sounds official."

"Sounds boring. So to celebrate me getting to stay, should we get Froyo?"

"Dad, don't call it that."

"Isn't that what all the kids are calling it?"

"No."

"Do you need to change before we go?"

"Let me just grab my sweats, and if you're not embarrassed to be seen with a swim rat, then I can go like this."

"I am not embarrassed to be seen with my talented daughter."

Between my coach and my mom, it felt like my dad was the only one who thought that. "I'll be right back." I went to my locker, pulled on my sweats, then shoved my wet towel in my duffel and slung the strap over my shoulder. When I got back outside, Jackson was standing next to my dad, talking to him like they were old friends. I slowed my hurried pace. As far as I knew, they'd never met before. Did Jackson even know it was my dad he was speaking to? Had Jackson been here the whole time?

"Moore," Jackson said when I reached them. "That was some excellent swimming. Not as good as my swim but a close second."

"You're a swimmer as well?" my dad asked.

"No, he's not," I answered before Jackson could.

He answered anyway, with a mocking tone. "I'm a bit of a novice. I came today to watch the experts and pick up a few pointers."

My dad, not realizing that everything that came out of Jackson's mouth was a joke, said, "That's nice. I'm sure Hadley will give you some pointers. We're going to get some Froyo right now. You should join us."

"Dad—" I started to scold when Jackson interrupted me with, "I'd love to."

I shot him a look that clearly said, *Stop being terrible and go away*, but it didn't faze him.

"Moore enjoys my company. She just told me the other day that she thought I was the funniest person she knew."

"Is that so?" my dad asked.

"He's actually the funniest person *he* knows."

"That too," Jackson said with a smile. "I'll meet you over there. The one on Coral Road?"

My dad nodded, and Jackson was gone.

"Dad, please don't invite people out with us before asking me."

"He was so pleasant and funny. I thought for sure you two must be friends."

We weren't friends. At all. He was annoying. My dad would soon find that out.

Only my dad wasn't finding out anything. Twenty minutes later and he was egging Jackson on—laughing at all his jokes, asking him questions to expand on his stories. My sugar-free yogurt wasn't distracting me well enough. Maybe I should've caved and gotten a few toppings.

"So then did he give you back your phone?" my dad asked after Jackson told him all about having his phone stolen at McDonald's, then calling it and having an hour-long conversation with the thief.

"No. Do you believe that? At the end of the conversation the guy said, 'I just arrived at the confessional. Great talking to you, man.' Then he hung up."

"So you made him feel guilty enough to go to church and confess but not guilty enough to return the phone?"

"I need to work on my skills."

I took the last bite of yogurt and dropped my spoon in my empty yogurt cup, hoping the noise would clue them both in that I was done. "Maybe he'd heard about the time you hid Gabriel's phone and made him go on a treasure hunt to find it. Your thief probably figured it was karma," I said.

Jackson laughed, then looked down at his cup, which was mostly candy bar toppings now swimming in half-melted yogurt. He'd been talking so much, he hadn't had time to eat it. "That's true. Maybe he had."

My dad clapped a hand on my back. "How come you haven't brought this boy home before? He's a riot."

"Because we don't really know each other." I tried to say it polite enough so that my dad wouldn't think I was being rude but blunt enough so that Jackson would get the message.

Jackson nodded. "It's true. We don't really know each other."

I stood up. "Well, I'm done. We should probably get going."

"I should go too," Jackson said. "I have things to do tonight."

We all walked outside together, and before we parted, my dad shook Jackson's hand. "Good to meet you. You should come to dinner some time."

"Dad, I'm sure Jackson is very busy."

Jackson met my eyes, then nodded at my dad. "She's right. Very busy."

"Everyone has to eat," Dad said.

Jackson laughed, then waved.

When my dad climbed into the truck and Jackson headed for his car, I opened the passenger door and said, "I'll be right back."

I caught Jackson just before he got to his car. "What's your deal?"

"What?"

"Why did you come today?"

"Your dad invited me."

"You could've said no."

"I didn't want to."

"Yeah, well, we're not friends. So . . ." Now I felt like I *was* being rude.

He smiled. "But we should be, Moore."

"That sounded creepy."

He laughed. "It did, didn't it? It wasn't supposed to." He opened his car door, which I just noticed belonged to a silver Lexus. Not surprising that he had a fancy car. He had the attitude of a kid who got handed everything. "You'd better get going."

He climbed in, shut the door, and started his engine.

"And you talk too much," I grumbled to his retreating

car. I walked back to the truck and got inside.

My dad had a leftover smile on his face. "I liked that kid."

"I could tell."

"He reminded me of . . ."

No, don't say it, don't say it, I mentally begged.

"Eric. I've never met someone who reminded me more of your brother."

TWELVE

was done obsessing over Heath Hall. I'd talked to him. He hadn't shown up to my swim meet the day before. As far as I was concerned my mission was accomplished. I didn't care who he was anymore. Amelia and I hadn't talked about him at all when we went out to eat earlier. We talked about what I thought her chances with DJ were (decent); we talked about who we thought would win awards at the swim banquet (the seniors); we talked about how Ms. Lin had accosted Amelia in the hall begging her to take another year of art (she nicely said no). But we had not talked about Heath Hall.

So why was I now pulling up his social media on my phone?

There wasn't a lot of activity on his part, but when I searched his name, I saw many people from the museum were congratulating him. He didn't need me to add to his ego. Besides, I'd already told him I liked the painting when I was there. In that back hallway. Where his hands were shaking and his eyes were darting.

He didn't have an ego, I realized. He had the exact opposite.

He wasn't some popular kid. He'd seemed so shaky, unsure of himself. Was that what this whole act of pretending to be a spy hero was about? It gave him confidence without having to be himself?

It didn't matter. I was done obsessing over Heath Hall. I tossed my phone into my desk drawer so I didn't drag it into the bathroom with me and went to get ready for bed.

After brushing my teeth and washing my face, I was in my room again, about to change into my pajamas, when I heard a muffled buzzing from the desk. I ignored it. I pulled a tank top and a pair of cotton shorts out of my drawer. I changed into them and dumped my dirty clothes into the hamper in the corner of my room under the poster of an Olympic-sized swimming pool taken at water level, from a swimmer's point of view. Bold black letters across the poster read: *Punish Your Goals.*

My phone buzzed again. I glanced at the drawer. What if Amelia was trying to get hold of me with some sort of best-friend emergency and I was just ignoring her need? I yanked open the drawer and pulled out my phone. It showed I had a notification: *DM@HeathHall.* I clicked on it.

My heart skipped a beat. Why would he message me? I sank down into my desk chair, then slid my finger over the screen until it hovered over the envelope icon.

A knock sounded at my door and I jumped. My mom poked her head inside the room.

"Hello. Came to say good night."

"Are you just getting home?" I asked.

"You know how meetings go. There's so much to discuss and delegate."

"Didn't you just have a meeting yesterday?"

"That was the sign-up meeting. This was the calendaring meeting."

I raised my eyebrows. "So many meetings."

"I know. I just wanted to tell you good job yesterday at your meet."

"Thank you."

"Also, I was thinking about that dress you wore to the museum Thursday night. That would be the perfect one to wear to the leukemia charity event on the twenty-fifth."

"The twenty-fifth?" I turned all the way around in my desk chair. She was still lingering in my doorway.

"Yes. Is there somewhere you'd rather be?" she asked.

"It's not that I'd rather be somewhere else, but we have a mandatory awards banquet at school for swim at the exact same time." Not to mention the charity dinner was about forty-five minutes away so it wasn't like I could make an appearance at both.

"I'm sure your coach would understand if you couldn't go."

Right. I could just use the *my brother is dead* card. It worked well. "He might let me out of it, but I also feel like I need to be there to support my teammates."

"And you don't feel like you need to support your family?"

"I've been every other year."

My mom started to speak but then stopped herself, donned her disappointed eyes, then said, "Well, think about it. Ultimately the decision is yours. You'll do the right thing."

That look made it seem like the decision wasn't mine at all, but I still said, "I'll think about it. Thanks."

"Good night, honey."

"Night."

My mom left, and I shut my bedroom door, then fell back onto my bed with a groan. My mom was right: the charity dinner was where I should go. But I couldn't help but think that being at the awards banquet would be important for the next year of swimming. For making sure Coach knew I wasn't just in this for me, that I supported the team. But my parents were important to me too. Why was this so hard?

I reached for my phone. I needed to talk to Amelia about this. She'd tell me what to do. I swiped across the screen of my phone. The direct message notification reminded me I had a message waiting. Instead of calling Amelia, I found myself clicking on the envelope icon.

Turns out I didn't want to swim again last night.

I stared at the message. Was he trying to get a reaction or was that his backward way of saying I didn't have to worry about him messing up a swim meet again? I thought about ignoring him but then typed: Control the urge for the final meet this year and I will have no problems with you.

As I moved to exit out of the screen, I saw the three

dots showing he was responding. I waited until it buzzed through.

So that is the only problem you have with me?

Was he looking for validation? He'd come to the wrong place. I typed back: That is the only thing I care about.

Swimming?

I narrowed my eyes. No, you disrupting my swimming.

Good to know.

Who are you? I needed to know who to avoid in real life.

I thought you already knew.

I knew he didn't really believe that. I'd given myself away at the museum when I'd chased him down and demanded his identity. No, you didn't. So . . . who are you?

Nice try.

What's it take to find out?

A need.

What does that even mean? I asked.

If you don't know what it means, then you don't have it.

We're talking in riddles now?

He didn't respond right away, and I found myself refreshing the page to make sure the site hadn't frozen. When nothing happened, I got up and pulled a pair of socks out of my dresser. I went to put on a sweatshirt and realized it was Robert's. I had forgotten to return it. I loved this sweatshirt and not because it was

Robert's—well, maybe a little because it was his—but because it was comfortable.

I folded it and put it on my desk. Then, maybe because I was mad that he wanted it back or maybe because I was tired of feeling like I was the only one still a little hung up on the relationship, I grabbed my perfume and sprayed the sweatshirt. If I had to return it, then he had to suffer through my scent for a few days. Hopefully it would stir up some memories that made him good and lonely. I spritzed it two more times for good measure, then shoved it in my backpack. That's when I remembered his other claim—that he'd left his math book here.

I moved to my hands and knees to search under my desk and bed. It wasn't in either of those places so I crawled over to the closet, where I had to sift through a layer of clothes on the floor—mostly T-shirts and jeans, my standard wardrobe. I came up empty-handed. I tried to remember the last time he'd done homework at my house and a picture of him sitting up against the far wall, his ankle on his knee, his pencil sideways in his mouth, came into my mind. "What'd you get for number four?" he'd asked through that pencil.

"I'm only on two."

"What's taking you so long?"

"I had to text Amelia the shoulder exercise I found."

"Of course you did," he'd mumbled.

My phone buzzed, bringing me out of my memory and reminding me I was still no closer to finding the math book. I stood up and sat on my bed, back against the headboard, and read the newest message from Heath Hall.

No riddles. Just truth.

That seemed like another riddle to me. I tried to interpret it. My brain was too tired to figure out his game. My mom had already messed with my head tonight to get me to go to the charity dinner. I didn't need more manipulation. I'd find out who he was at some point. Someone would slip. I remembered part of a quote my dad once told me. Something about how truth couldn't be hidden. I quickly Googled it, then typed it out for Heath Hall.

Three things cannot be long hidden: the sun, the moon, and the truth.

His response was quick. Too quick to have been Googled like mine.

Man is least himself when he talks in his own person. Give him a mask, and he will tell you the truth.

You have the mask. What's your truth?

Exactly.

Had I figured something out? Had he offered some sort of truth at the museum with that mask on? That he liked to paint? Who in our school liked to paint? I copied and pasted his quote into the search engine on my computer and it showed it was from Oscar Wilde. Who wrote it probably wasn't significant—the quote itself was what fit his situation perfectly—but it was nice to know who had originally said it.

A quiet knock sounded at my door.

"Yes?"

It creaked open, revealing my dad. "I thought I heard you up in here. It's late."

"Yeah, I was just about to go to sleep."

"Mom told me you might not come to the charity dinner this year."

My mom and dad were different. If a person heard about my brother's death from my dad, they would probably assume he had died years ago. If they heard about it from my mom, they would most likely assume he'd died months ago. So it was much easier for me to talk to my dad about things like this. "It's the same night as my awards banquet for swim."

"That's a hard choice."

The problem was that if there were nobody else's feelings involved but my own, there would be no choice. But that wasn't the case. "I think I should support my swim team."

"I understand why you'd want to. That's a big part of your life."

"But I want to be there for you guys too."

He smiled. "Like I said, it's a hard choice. You'll make the right one." With that, he nodded his head at my phone and added, "Lights out in five."

"Okay."

He shut the door and I sighed. I wasn't so sure I would make the right decision because as of now I was leaning toward the awards banquet and I had a feeling that even my dad assumed I'd go to the dinner. After all, it was family . . . and seventeen years of tradition.

I turned my attention back to my phone. **You want to know a truth? Choices suck.**

What choices?

What was I doing? I didn't even know this person. My frustration at my situation almost made me vent about my personal life to a complete stranger. Not just any stranger but someone who was in the habit of selfishly disrupting other people's lives.

Nothing. Good night.

He answered: You should always make the choice that's best for you.

Of course he'd say that. That's what *he* did, thought about himself. And besides, even if I went with his advice, I wasn't sure which choice was best for me. One would be right for me now and one later. And I didn't even know which was which. I turned off my phone and put it on my desk. I wasn't sure I'd make the right choice but I did know that I'd have to make one.

THIRTEEN

I pulled the sweatshirt out of my backpack and handed it to Robert. I'd flagged him down in the hall after I saw him leaving the science building. "Here. I couldn't find your math book."

"Oh. I found my math book. Thanks." He held the sweatshirt to his nose. "It smells like you."

My face got hot. "Yeah. It's been at my house." Under a couple sprays of my perfume. "Where was your math book?" I asked, mostly to change the subject.

"At Luke's."

"I looked for it the other night. It brought back some homework memories."

"You mean like the time when I did my homework and you Googled swim strokes," he said flatly.

"Right." It was nice of him to keep reminding me why we weren't together anymore. "Me and my one-track mind," I added sarcastically.

"So you're admitting it for once?"

A new song came out of the earbuds that were dangling around my neck. I could barely make out the tune but my mind immediately started singing the lyrics. I wanted to just put them in and walk away. "I guess the truth can't be hidden forever," I said, mostly because I didn't want to argue about this.

"Or the sun or the moon."

I froze. "What?"

"Is that not how the saying goes? Your dad said that to us once, right?" His expression was innocent, relaxed. It didn't seem like he was hiding anything or trying to fool me.

"He did?"

"Yes, you'd shown up late for curfew and we made up some excuse that he obviously knew was a lie."

I could remember my dad giving me a lecture, but I didn't remember Robert being there at all. I tried to picture Robert in a tux and a mask. At the museum Heath Hall had been forty feet away, so it was hard to gauge size. If I backed up forty feet right now maybe it would be easier to tell.

"Why are you looking at me like that?"

"Like what?"

"Like I just ate your last french fry."

"You liked to do that a lot."

He smiled. "Only because it made you mad."

I took a step back. "I have to go."

He said something behind me that I didn't hear because I was immediately surrounded by the chaos of the school hallway and my music. For a moment I didn't remember where I was supposed to be next. When Amelia joined me, I realized it was lunchtime.

"Have we ruled out Robert?" I asked, turning off my music.

"For dating again? Making out with? Talking to? I need some context here."

"No, as Heath Hall."

"We mentioned Robert as a possibility but decided he isn't the putting-on-a-mask-in-a-public-place-for-attention type. Why?"

As we walked to our normal spot in the courtyard, I summarized my conversation with Heath Hall and my conversation with Robert a few minutes ago, including the quote he'd said. The same one from the other night.

"You're still having private conversations with Heath Hall?"

"Yes."

"So . . . you think it's Robert?"

It didn't make sense. Robert wasn't in any way, shape, or form an artist, which was the only real clue I had about Heath Hall. I let out a long sigh. "I don't know. I don't care. I don't know why I'm still thinking about this."

"I don't either. Our list was pretty much obliterated after almost all of them were at the museum, watching the events unfold. And you were able to talk to fake Heath about the pool thing. I thought you'd be over it."

"I am." I was. I was definitely going to be. We sat down at the table and I let my backpack slide to the ground next to me. "Oh! I keep forgetting to tell you." I couldn't believe I hadn't told Amelia what my dad had said about Jackson yet. Amelia would tell me it wasn't so bad. That Jackson wasn't that horrible and that it meant nothing about how I would've gotten along with Eric.

"What happened?" she asked. "You look miserable."

"Jackson."

"I don't understand. How did Jackson happen? Is that

like a metaphor or something? Are we using Jackson as a verb now?"

I smiled. "I can think of several words where the name Jackson would fit perfectly in their place."

She moved her eyebrows up and down. "I'm sure you can."

I smacked her arm. "They would be bad words, not good ones."

"So. Tell me how you got Jacksoned."

"He squirmed his way into hanging out with me and my dad at the yogurt place."

She grabbed my arm in faux horror. "How awful."

"It was! He made my dad like him."

She pulled out her bagged lunch. "How did he do that?"

"Basically he didn't stop talking the entire time and told a million stories that made him sound funny and charming. I have a feeling this is all part of some elaborate joke he's put together."

She laughed. "Jackson flirting with you is part of a joke?"

"He wasn't flirting."

"I know you don't have a flirt meter like the rest of us, but I promise you he was."

I opened my mouth to tell her what my dad had said when she added, "You do not need to give in to him, though. I like him just fine, but I can see why you don't."

I shut my mouth. "You can?"

"Yeah. He's pretty self-absorbed and childish. He makes me laugh, but I could never take him seriously."

"Right . . . exactly." It felt weird admitting that. It felt like admitting that I wouldn't have liked my brother. And apparently Amelia wouldn't have liked him either.

"What's wrong?" she asked.

"Nothing." Absolutely nothing.

"Did you bring a lunch?" she asked, nodding toward my bag.

I stood. "Yes, but I need to go talk to Coach. I'm not going to the awards banquet." I had just decided this, and although three people had told me I'd make the right decision, it didn't feel right. My stomach was twisted tighter than it was prerace. I figured either decision would've produced that feeling, though, so I didn't change my mind.

"It's mandatory," Amelia said.

"For people without dead brothers."

"I hate you."

"I know. If only we could all be so lucky." I felt a twinge of guilt for joking about it, but sometimes it was all I could do to lighten up the whole subject. And besides, if my brother was as "fun" as my dad claimed, he would probably find the exchange amusing.

"I thought you *wanted* to go to the awards banquet. Cement your place as favorite with the coach."

I picked up my bag. "I did, but I've been thinking, and maybe I am too singly focused."

"Did Robert get in your head? I'll kill him."

"No. Well, sort of, but I started it. I do think a lot about swimming. My life kind of revolves around it."

"Mine would too if I were as awesome as you."

"Thanks, but even if I were that awesome, it's no excuse to be so obsessed."

"I think any excuse is a good one to be obsessed."

I smiled, took a step away, then said, "You okay here . . . ?"

She rolled her eyes and nodded to a table behind her. "I'll go sit with Katie. Good luck with the coach's wrath."

"Dead brother," I called as I walked away.

I knocked on the glass outside Coach's door when I arrived, even though I could see that it wasn't Coach inside but DJ. I bit my lip. We still weren't exactly back to pre-insult comfort around each other, but I knew he felt bad, so I was trying to get past it. DJ gestured me in.

"Hey, is Coach around?" I asked.

"He had a lunch meeting with a parent."

"Sounds fun."

"Can I help you with something?"

"No . . . Well, actually I was just going to tell him that I can't go to the awards banquet. You want to pass on that message for me?"

He laughed. "Nice try."

"I'll give you a dollar."

"Tempting but still no. You know it's mandatory, right? I don't think you'll be able to get out of it if you plan on swimming next year."

I thought about telling DJ about Eric. Oh, who was I kidding? DJ probably already knew. It seemed everyone did. I knew having a dead brother had gotten me an extra bit of something—food in the lunch line, percentage points on grades, days for makeup work—over the years. I was sure everybody knew that too. The only thing I could be 100 percent sure I'd earned was my swimming times. The clock wasn't subjective. Nobody could change that.

I shrugged. "He'll be mad, but my conflict is important too."

He picked up a pen and clicked the end. "I'll leave him a message that you were here. Maybe he'll call you out of your next class to talk."

"Sounds good."

"By the way, thanks for letting me tag along at the

museum the other night."

I nodded. "We kind of ditched you for a while."

"I'm kind of a loner anyway."

"Meaning you'd rather be alone or that people tend to leave you alone?"

"Both."

I tugged on the straps of my backpack. "So you had fun?"

"I love art."

"What was your favorite piece there?"

"Did you see the aquarium sculpture on the second floor?"

"No."

"It was amazing. It looked real."

"We were a little preoccupied that night."

"I noticed. With what?"

I didn't want to admit it out loud. I was embarrassed that we had ever taken the Heath Hall thing seriously. "Something stupid. But anyway, I'll let you get back to whatever you were doing."

"Hadley," he said before I could leave.

I paused with my hand on the doorknob. "Yeah?"

"I think you should try, like really try, to come to the awards banquet. You'll be glad you did."

I nodded because I didn't feel like arguing, or telling

him my parents had basically said the same thing about their event. That everybody seemed to think their thing was the most important, the most worth my time, the thing that I would be happier to attend. At this point, I wanted to skip both.

FOURTEEN

"Hey, Ms. Lin." I stood in the art room after swim practice the next day, taking in all the paintings around me.

"Hadley, hello. What brings you here? Have you decided to add art to your schedule after all?"

As my mentor teacher, Ms. Lin was in charge of helping me figure out my four-year goals and I always thought she felt cheated that she got the one person in the whole school probably the least interested in art.

"Nope. Still not even a little bit artistic."

"There's an artist inside each of us."

"I think I drowned mine."

She gave a courtesy laugh, then said, "So what brings you here? Did you already fill out your schedule for next year?"

We'd gotten the sheets that morning. I liked to get things off my to-do list as quickly as possible. "Yes." I handed it to her.

While she looked over it, my eyes continued to wander the room. Art hung on the walls and paintings were drying on easels. I bit my lip. "Did any of your students show a piece at the museum on Tenth Street for the show last week? I saw a painting there that my parents might want to buy." This wasn't the reason I had filled out my schedule so fast. I was not still curious about who Heath Hall was. Or at least that's what I was telling myself.

She brightened at my mention of going to the museum. "Sounds like you didn't drown your creative side, after all."

"It's for my parents," I said again before she whipped out an eraser and started changing my schedule.

"Students don't have to get my approval to enter pieces there. They have to submit them for consideration like everyone else. Did the piece not have a name with it?"

"No." And I knew for a fact the piece had been snuck in and not submitted for consideration at all.

"What did it look like?"

"It was a painting of a shipwreck in the middle of the ocean." It was dark and alive and even thinking about it now gave me goose bumps again. Maybe I did have a creative side clawing for air somewhere inside of me.

"I haven't seen a piece like that come through my class. But most serious students work on paintings at home too."

"Who would you say your most talented student is?"

"Everyone is an artist in their own way. I don't pick favorites."

I laughed. "I won't tell anyone."

She looked around, as if to make sure we were still alone, and led me to the far corner of the room where a half-done painting sat. Even incomplete, it was gorgeous. It was a tree, twisted and gnarled, dark and perfect. It had the same feel as the ocean scene from the museum. The same strokes or depth or something. "Yes. Who painted this?"

"I'm not allowed to tell you that without his permission. But I'll ask him if he's interested in selling any of his work. I'll be in touch."

"Okay. Thanks, Ms. Lin." He'd know why I was asking. We'd been face-to-face in that hallway at the museum. We'd chatted online. He wouldn't let Ms. Lin tell me who he was.

The door to the art room flew open and I whirled around.

"Hey, Ms. Lin. I heard you needed some muscle in here." Jackson walked into the room.

Ms. Lin smiled like he was the cutest thing in the world. I curled my lip but then smoothed my hair, all too aware that I had just gotten out of the pool. Not that I cared what he thought of me, but still.

Jackson noticed me, and his mouth twisted into a sly smile. "Oh, I see you already have plenty of muscle. Never mind." He started to back out of the room.

"No, Jackson," Ms. Lin said. "Hadley was just here turning in her schedule. I still need your help."

"Moore. We keep running into each other. It's almost like you're following me."

He wanted me to point out that I was in here first. I wasn't going to do that.

"I didn't know you liked art," I said to Jackson.

"There's an artist inside each of us," he said with a wink in Ms. Lin's direction.

"So which painting is yours?" I asked.

"My artist just moves around other people's paintings."

Ms. Lin began pointing to some easels that Jackson immediately folded and moved to the far end of the room. "I asked for a student council member to help me stack paintings once a week and Jackson answered the call."

"I am a call answerer. People call, I answer."

"Yeah, got it."

"Do you really get it? How about one more iteration? If I answer, it means someone has called."

Yes, he was still the most annoying person on the planet.

"Maybe you'll have the desire to paint by being around the paintings," Ms. Lin said to him like she'd had this conversation with him before. So he obviously wasn't the artist responsible for the piece in the corner.

As I moved to leave, my dad's words about my brother being like Jackson came back to me. Dad could've compared Eric to almost anyone else and I would've been fine. But Jackson? Maybe I just didn't know him well enough. Maybe he had another side. But that wouldn't matter. My dad had met only this side. And this was the side that reminded him of my brother. If I hung out with Jackson more, would I get used to him? Would this over-the-top personality become endearing?

Jackson lifted an easel over his head. "You need a body model for class, Ms. Lin? I've been told my physique is nearly perfect."

Nope. That would never become endearing. This

sucked because before, being around Jackson was only an irritation, but now it was depressing. My stomach hurt, my chest hurt, my head hurt. Why had my dad said that? It tainted all the things I had learned about Eric over the years.

"What did I do?" Jackson asked, and I realized I was staring. I could feel the scowl on my face and I quickly smoothed it back to uninterested.

"Nothing. See you later, Ms. Lin."

"Wait up," Jackson called as I left the classroom.

I walked faster but he still caught up with me. I gave myself a mental pep talk. I could be nice to Jackson. He was a nice guy. He was just helping Ms. Lin. That's what nice guys did. "I thought you were moving easels."

"I'm finished. She only had a few for me to stack today."

"Lucky me."

"So I have a serious question for you."

Did Jackson know how to be serious? "I'm listening."

"Was Amelia your ride home?"

"Um . . . yes. Why?" I turned to him, now wary.

"Because isn't that her?" He pointed to the street, where I saw her yellow car, its tiny blinker going on and off, indicating she was turning left.

Why was she leaving me? I'd told her I needed to drop off my schedule and that it would only be a minute. She took longer than me in the locker room, so it shouldn't have been a problem even if it had been more like fifteen minutes. "Did you tell her to leave me?"

Jackson's eyes twinkled in amusement. "Why would I do that?"

"Why do you do anything?" I said more to myself, then pulled out my phone to see ten texts littering my screen. All from Amelia.

The light turned green and she turned. I called her but she didn't answer.

"You're in luck, Moore. I can drive you."

"That's okay. I'll walk."

"You'd rather walk than let me drive you?"

That did sound kind of stupid, but I wanted to answer yes. It was only two miles away.

"My car is dying to drive you home. This has nothing to do with me. You wouldn't deny my car what it wants, right? It just got out of the shop."

"Why was your car in the shop?"

"My friend thought it would be funny to see what would happen if he put milk in the gas tank. I probably don't have to tell you that it did not end well."

I laughed.

"Oh, now you laugh."

"I just think it's funny when you're on the other end of pranks for once."

"My life was endangered."

I laughed again. "Milk is noncombustible. I'm sure it screwed up your car but you were safe."

"You know about cars?"

"Not really." Not like my brother. He and my dad had restored his truck from the engine block up. I knew my dad missed talking cars with someone, so sometimes I would humor him. "Do you?"

"Not a thing."

This thought relieved me. It was a way he wasn't like Eric.

"This makes you happy, for some reason? Do you hate cars?"

"No. It's nothing."

"So? A ride?"

"Sure. Why not?" Maybe I would learn a few more things about him that would make him different from my brother.

"This is your car?" I asked as we approached a beige sedan. It was at least twenty years old and looked like a car my grandpa would drive.

"You don't like my Buick Century? It's a classic."

"No, this cannot claim that title."

"You're going to hurt his feelings." He stuck the key in the lock, turned it twice to the left, once to the right, then jiggled it before pulling it back out and opening the door. I wasn't sure if that was really necessary or if it was just something he did as a joke.

"I thought you had a Lexus."

"Who wants a Lexus when they have the opportunity to drive this?"

"True."

"That was my dad's car. He let me borrow it a few times while my car was getting fixed."

"Oh." I climbed in and spent the entire time he walked around the car trying to buckle my seat belt.

"That one doesn't work," he said as he sat down. He patted the middle seat. "Guess you'll have to sit next to me."

"Did you break this seat belt on purpose?"

"Best pickup line ever, right? I wish I had thought of it on my own. But no, I didn't. It legitimately broke all by itself."

"Right." I slid over next to him and buckled up.

He draped his arm across the back of the seat, lifted one side of his mouth into a half smile, and met my eyes. "Hey." His eyes were green. Like my brother's.

I scowled, and he laughed and put both hands on the wheel.

"Sorry, I'll behave. It was just a joke," he said.

Of course it was.

"Where to?" he asked, starting the engine.

I told him where I lived, then reached for the radio.

"It doesn't work."

I gasped. "How can you drive without music?"

"Well, it might be an old-car thing, but my gas pedal isn't connected to the radio at all."

"Funny. It's just, I wouldn't be able to do that."

"But to be fair, you don't do anything without music."

"Music is life." It was to me at least. It filled me up, gave me words, helped me to feel or not to feel.

"Interesting."

"What?"

"Nothing."

It wasn't until we were almost to my house that I remembered my brother's truck up there on the platform like a trophy in our front yard. I knew the whole town knew the story behind it, but people still had this need to hear it from me. They wanted the details. And they'd ask in this soft, sad voice. I wasn't ready to hear that voice from Jackson because it would sound even more fake than when other people did it.

A sharp pain shot through my right shoulder. I clutched at it, then pinched the muscle, hoping to soothe it faster.

"What's the matter?"

"I just get shoulder cramps every once in a while."

"From swimming?"

I gritted my teeth as a new wave of pain surged through

my shoulder. "Yes." And they seemed to be happening more frequently, which worried me.

"Is there anything I can—"

"No, I'm good." And I was. A minute later my shoulder relaxed and so did I. Until I remembered the truck in my front yard as we pulled up to the house.

"Wow. Awesome truck," Jackson said.

My brows shot down as I studied his happy, innocent expression.

"I see why you weren't impressed with my classic. Your dad has restored a real one to perfection." He turned off the engine and hopped out. Next thing I knew, he was walking around my brother's truck, running his hand along the paint job like it was a rare gem.

"Can I sit in it?"

"No!"

"Your dad doesn't let people touch it?"

Had he really never seen it before? We didn't live on a busy street. If he had no need to come into this neighborhood, I could see why he might not have ever seen it. "Have you never heard . . . ?" Did this mean he didn't know about my brother?

"What? Am I missing something? Did your dad win some big award for this or something? I'm always a step behind in this town."

It took me two seconds to remember that he moved

here his freshman year. I assumed people still talked about my family. About my brother. But maybe we were old news. It was kind of ironic that the one person in town who reminded my dad of my brother didn't even know of Eric's existence. The thought of someone not knowing about my brother made my breath catch in my throat. Did the thought thrill me or devastate me? I wasn't sure.

"It's complicated."

He held up his hands. "Hey, I get it. If I had this truck, I wouldn't want people touching it either."

"Right. Well, thanks for the ride."

"I told you we were going to be friends, Moore."

I wanted to object, but I just smiled and headed for my house.

FIFTEEN

B ungee jumping? Your activities have quite a range.
I tapped my fingers lightly on the keyboard, waiting for a fast response from Heath Hall like I'd gotten the other night, but was left with lots of white screen waiting to be filled with message bubbles. He couldn't be online all the time. I shouldn't have gotten on the computer the second I walked in the door anyway. I should've called Amelia and yelled at her for ditching me.

So I did.

"What took you so long?" she responded.

"I started asking Ms. Lin about the best artists she taught."

"For the Heath Hall thing again?"

"Yes."

"And did you find out anything?"

"Nope. She acted like she had some legal contract to keep names secret. Kind of like all the people who know who Heath Hall is and won't say."

"Well, don't forget there are a bunch of people who just say whatever random name they think of too."

"That's probably part of his game."

"True. I'm sorry I couldn't wait for you. I tried to text you that, but you must not have gotten it."

"No, I got them. Too late. So your aunt is in town?"

"Yes, and my mom wanted me to come straight home after practice."

"Aunt Faye?"

"The very one. It should be a fun week," she said in a monotone voice. "Oh." Her voice was back to its animated self. "Guess what I saw online just now?"

"That Heath Hall is going to bungee jump this weekend?"

"You saw that too?"

"Yes."

"So are we going to witness another Heath Hall event?" she asked.

"I don't know. I mean, what's the point? I'm sure he'll be wearing a mask again."

"The point is that we have nothing better to do and it's obvious that you really want to know who he is, despite what you're saying."

She was right. I did want to know. I'd been trying to deny it or write it off as curiosity, but it was more than that. "I'm worried it's someone I actually know. For that second I thought it was Robert, I was terrified."

"Why?"

"I don't want to be blindsided. Caught off guard. I don't like secrets. At least not when other people are keeping them."

"It's your controlling nature."

"I'm not controlling."

She ignored my protest. "Maybe his mask will fall off as he's flying through the air. Or maybe when he hits the water."

"Hardly anyone hits the water off that bridge. Did you?"

"No." Bungee jumping off Whitestone Bridge wasn't anything new or special. Practically everyone I knew had done it. It was even professionally run by a company called Just Jump that swept in when it became popular. So I wasn't sure why Heath Hall was making a point of doing it. He had given a speech at the museum about his reasons for displaying the painting. Sure it was a little, tiny, barely-worth-mentioning speech but maybe he'd do something similar before jumping.

"I really hope I can come. I will start wearing down my mom now, but with the swim meet all day and my aunt here, she's probably going to want me home. She likes me as a buffer."

"More like a hostage."

"Exactly. I'll talk to you soon." She hung up.

I heard my mom come in the garage door. She was midsentence and I figured she was on the phone but I went out to greet her anyway. She waved at me with one hand, her keys, hooked around one of those fingers, jingling as she did. Her other arm held groceries while her cell phone was precariously pushed against her ear by her raised shoulder. I grabbed the bag from her and her hand took over the job of holding the phone.

"So can we count on you for a donation, then?" She waited and I held my breath along with her. "That's great," she finally said. "I'll send you the forms." She hung up with a smile. "We're almost fully funded."

"That's awesome. This is like record time."

"Every time it gets easier. That's the reward of experience." She gave me a hug. "How was school?"

"Average."

She smiled. "Are you already anticipating the end of swim season?"

"I'm going to be so bored when it's over."

She pulled on the ends of my hair. "Well, even if you don't like the break, your hair likes it."

"Thanks a lot."

She laughed and started unloading the groceries, handing me a few items to put away as she went.

I ended up at the far counter, dumping a bag of rice into a canister that sat right beneath the keys to my brother's truck. During the seven seconds it took to complete the task, I found myself staring at those keys. For a split second I imagined ripping them out of the box and hurling them against the wall. The thought surprised me. I pressed the lid back on the canister and turned my back to the keys.

"I got stuck at school today," I breathed out.

"How?"

"Amelia couldn't give me a ride home."

"You should've called."

"A friend . . ." I caught myself when I imagined how smug Jackson's smile would be if he heard me say that. "Well . . . not really a friend but this guy I know gave me a ride home."

"That was nice of him. Tell him thank you."

What would be nice would be if I had a car. How come I couldn't say that out loud? "I'm going to the charity dinner," I said instead. It wasn't a good instead. It was a bad instead. It was an instead that gave my mom what she wanted and expressed none of my frustration.

She clapped her hands and rose up on her toes. "Oh, I knew you would. I'm so happy." She hugged me again. Her hair smelled like vanilla and lilacs. She pushed me out by my shoulders. "Your coach called about it and we had a long chat."

"Coach called?" I guess DJ gave him the message about why I wanted to talk to him, after all. *Thank you, DJ.* I owed him a dollar.

"Yes, and I know he wanted us to be at the banquet, but he understands."

"He does? He wasn't mad?"

"Of course not. You'll have so many award ceremonies in the future. Ones that don't conflict with other important dates."

She was right. I would. I nodded and then wandered off to my room while she hummed happily in the kitchen.

I clicked on my music, the sound immediately stilling my mind. My computer was open on my desk. I swiped my finger across the trackpad to wake it up and it dinged with a notification.

Heath Hall is a man of many talents, he'd written in response to my claim that his activities seemed to have a wide range.

I sat at my desk. I wouldn't exactly call bungee jumping a talent.

Really?

Not even close. Now that painting, that was talent.

Well, good thing it's not about showing off talents, then.

What is it about?

After a long pause that had me wondering if he was going to answer at all, he said, Facing fears. Expressing secrets. Discovering truth.

Expressing secrets? That seems to be the exact opposite of what you do.

True.

That answer was maddening. I thought back to the museum when he had said he'd always feared showing his art in public. That was a fear and now he was facing another one?

So what? You're afraid of heights? Of falling?

This time he didn't answer my question. He asked one. Do you have any fears?

The cursor blinked on the screen, over and over. It seemed to blink in time to the beat of the song playing over my speakers. Of course I had fears. Too many. Ones

I didn't want to think about. The song ended and silence filled my room. My chest constricted. When a new song started, I blew out a breath.

I can't think of anything. Spiders?

SIXTEEN

I stood outside the chain-link fence, staring at the crowded pool the next day, a scowl on my face. Coach had given us the afternoon off, and I figured it was because he'd wanted us to have a rest day before the meet, but maybe it was because he had to give up the pool. When had water polo started? That was a fall sport. Did they have a spring league I didn't know about? I hated sharing the pool with other people. The reminder that it wasn't just my pool was a hard one to accept.

I tromped back to my dad's truck that I had borrowed. I could go do an ocean swim but the waves screwed up my timing. There was a lake I frequented but it was only April so it would be freezing. As I started my drive home, however, my body itched. It felt like it was on fire. I needed to swim. I could handle cold.

It was a twenty-minute drive to my favorite spot. I parked in a dirt lot and took the trail that would be my stomping ground this summer. A trail I was pretty sure I had single-handedly made the summer before. I stepped out of my shoes, taking in the trees that surrounded the lake. I couldn't imagine a more beautiful place to swim. The sky was bright blue and there was a part between the deep green trees and hills where it touched the water that made it seem like I could swim past the edge of the lake and continue into the sky forever.

I took off my sweats and stepped into the water. It was even colder than I had imagined it would be, taking my breath away. I went to click on my music but stopped myself. I could prove I was able to be alone with my own thoughts. I threw my cap and player on top of my sweats, submerged myself in the water, then floated on my back, staring at the sky. I lay there, the water slowly numbing my skin, seeping into my ears, muffling sound. I let my arms and legs drift. I had to force myself not to do a single stroke.

It had been years since I'd been in water without swimming. Not since I was a kid. The sky above felt like it was sitting on my chest. My final swim meet of the season was coming up. And then my brother's benefit. Maybe I could set a personal record at my swim meet. That might help dampen some of the sad feelings my parents would surely feel at the benefit.

Every two seconds my arm twitched, my brain trying to make it do what it did every time it was here. After sixty more seconds I gave up and swam. As if to punish myself for the small break, I swam twice as long.

What do you do for fun? That was the question waiting for me from Heath Hall after dinner that night. Did he think we were chatting buddies now? Maybe if we were, he would slip up and give away who he was. I could keep chats surface level. Only saying things everyone already knew about me.

Swim. I typed even though my shoulders were telling me otherwise at the moment, sitting under a couple of ice packs.

No, I said for fun.

That is fun for me. What about you?

He seemed good at keeping chats surface level too, though. Or avoiding questions altogether. Swimming is fun for you? It seems like work.

I don't get paid for it.

Is that the only way you measure work?

Is there another way? I asked.

Putting more into something than you get out of it.

So he thought I put more into swimming than I got out of it? Why did everyone assume that? Why was everyone always trying to talk me out of something that made me happy? I typed my response. **So by that definition, does that mean fun is getting more out of something than you put into it?**

Absolutely.

I don't know that I agree with that. Sometimes hard work brings a sense of accomplishment that feels amazing.

That just proved my definition of work, not disproved it. So what do you do for fun?

Did this line of questioning give me any hints as to who Heath Hall was? Obviously someone who thought I swam too much. There were probably a lot of people who thought that. It didn't really narrow it down much. **Today I stared at the sky. It took zero effort and I got a lot out of it.** That was only half true. It actually took me a lot of effort to stare at that sky. It still felt a little like it was sitting on my chest.

What did you get out of it?

Looking at the sky?

Yes.

I lied: Relaxation.

★ ★ ★

This was the second time I found myself outside the art room this week after practice. The first time had produced no leads. But this one had. My heart was pounding as I waited to cut him off as he came out. I still couldn't believe he was in there. I had no idea he liked art. But he couldn't be Heath Hall. We'd ruled him out. Why would it be him? When we chatted the other day online, Heath had said that the mask was about keeping secrets. Had he kept this huge secret from me for months when we were together? It didn't seem possible. It wasn't.

It felt like I'd been waiting forever. Finally, the door squeaked open, and I stepped in the path like I had been on my way in.

"Hadley," he said in surprise.

"Robert. Hi. What are you doing?"

Was Robert Heath Hall? Things that had happened over the last couple weeks flashed through my mind. The fact that he remembered the truth quote, the fact that he was acting shifty when we were talking about it, the fact that I hadn't seen him at all at the museum, the fact that he thought I swam too much. Maybe I had ruled him out too soon.

"Just talking to Ms. Lin."

I looked at his hands for any evidence of paint. "You

talked to her about a painting?"

"What? No. My schedule. She's my mentor. Isn't she yours too?"

"Oh yeah, right." A seed of doubt at my theory wedged itself in my mind. "Well, I was going to talk to her about a painting. Remember at the art museum?"

"Right, for that Heath Hall thing." He didn't even flinch when he said it. Did that mean he was practiced at pretending it wasn't him or that it really wasn't him?

"Yes. Well, I loved the painting he did. I was hoping to buy it."

He laughed, low at first and then loud.

I crossed my arms. So he was Heath Hall. Why else would he be laughing like this? He knew he had fooled me and now he got to rub it in. My cheeks heated in embarrassment.

"You only want to buy it because you think it'll help you learn his identity."

Oh. Or there was that. He knew my true motives. "Why won't you just tell me?"

His mocking smile softened. "You're getting closer."

"So is it one of your friends?"

"No, it's not."

"Someone I already know?"

"Sort of."

I huffed. What did that mean? "For the record, I really

do like his painting. It's amazing."

His leftover smile fully dropped off his face now, and he reached out and grabbed my hand as I turned to go, jerking me to a halt. He spun me back toward him. "You want to catch a movie Saturday?"

"Saturday? I might've, but I'll be following Heath Hall to Whitestone Bridge and watching him jump. Maybe if you told me who he was we could catch that movie." That was a bluff. I didn't want to catch a movie with Robert. Nothing had changed with either of us since our breakup and nothing was going to. My butterflies were completely squashed and I was happy for it.

He tapped my chin with his closed fist like he had suddenly turned into my grandpa or something. "Nice try."

Nice try. That sounded familiar. Heath Hall had said that to me in our chat online. I narrowed my eyes, shook my head, and walked away.

I hate Robert, I texted Amelia.

Do I need to kill him again?

He's just frustrating.

Are you almost here? Remember the whole my-aunt-is-in-town thing? I'll have to strand you again if you don't get to the parking lot. Why are you always going on these missions without me?

I reached her car and opened the passenger door. "Because you take twenty minutes to leave the locker room and I take five, that's why."

"I feel like I haven't seen you all week."

"Because you haven't."

"Well, you get this ten-minute car ride to fill me in on everything."

"Ten minutes is not enough."

"Then you'd better talk fast."

First I told her about Robert and the conversation we just had, finishing with, "Then he asked me out. Do you believe he asked me out?"

"Deflection!"

"What?"

"He's Heath Hall."

"What?"

"He was trying to shock you into forgetting your accusations."

"I don't know. If he is, he's the best actor in the world, and I never considered him all that good at lying."

"We'll see Saturday, won't we? Maybe you should call him and say you've changed your mind. That you want to go out with him Saturday. Then if Heath Hall doesn't show up because he's out with you at the movies, we'll know for sure."

That wasn't a bad idea. It wasn't really a good idea either. Because if Robert wasn't Heath Hall, then I'd be stuck at the movies with Robert.

"How about we both go to the bridge, and while we're watching Heath Hall, I call Robert on the phone."

"Yes. Brilliant. Then you don't actually have to go out with the loser."

She pulled up in front of my house. "I will sit here for five more minutes and face the wrath of my mother for one more story."

I wanted to talk about the Jackson/Eric connection that was still plaguing me. I hadn't told her before and now I was regretting it. But that would take more than five minutes. I needed her full attention and her advice and I wanted to be able to vent for as long as I needed. So I settled for the other story I hadn't told her yet. "When you abandoned me at school the other day, Jackson drove me home."

"Home? Here?"

"No, one of my other five homes. Yes, of course here."

"So you had to tell him the story of the truck?" How was that the first thing she thought of when it didn't even cross my mind until we were almost to my house? Maybe because I saw it every day and it was as common to me as the grass or the driveway or the mailbox.

"That's the thing. I didn't have to tell him. He just assumed it was my dad's and I let him."

"Wait, he doesn't know about your brother?"

"I guess not."

"You don't think that's going to be weird when he's talking to your dad and it comes up?"

"Why would he be talking to my dad?"

"I don't know. Why did he talk to your dad before?"

I groaned.

"It'll be fine. Just tell him . . . or don't. It's not like you're friends. Now, out of my car. Aunt Faye awaits."

"Have you asked your mom about the bungee jump event? You're going to be able to come, right?"

"I will be there. Even if I have to bring my aunt with me."

SEVENTEEN

brought my headphones to the meet this time. But no matter how loud the music was, as I sat on the cold cement bench, elbows on my knees, I couldn't block out the fact that Jackson and my dad were sitting in the stands together. Why was he at the swim meet anyway? I scanned the group of guys warming up for the next race. Was one of his friends on the swim team?

He was going to ask about the truck. My dad was going to tell him about my brother. Then my dad would think I was ashamed to talk about it or too sad to tell the story. And Jackson would think I was a liar. It didn't matter. Amelia was right. Even if Jackson wanted to be, we weren't friends.

I concentrated on the ground beneath my feet. I couldn't think about this right now. I had a race to swim. My last one. Of the entire season. And I was going to be distracted. I clasped my hands behind my head, my forearms pushing my earphones in even more.

A hand on my shoulder had me sitting up straight. It was DJ, saying something I couldn't hear. I turned off my player.

"What?"

"Are your shoulders okay? You look like you're in pain."

They were killing me. "No. I mean, yes, they're fine. I'm just trying to get in the zone."

"You don't want to ice them for a little while? You probably have twenty minutes before you need to warm up for your next swim."

"Yes, I should go sit in the office for a little while." Out of sight, out of mind. That's how I hoped it would work.

He walked with me toward the building. "You've been swimming great today."

"Thank you."

"You're definitely on track for a scholarship."

"I hope so."

We arrived at the office, and he strapped a bag of ice onto each shoulder. The cold seeped into my skin and I relaxed a bit.

"I guess they were tighter than I thought. Thank you, DJ . . . DJ . . . What does that stand for?" I laid my cheek on one of my shoulders, letting the ice cool my cheeks that seemed to be a little warm now too.

"Let's just say that I go by DJ for a reason."

"A name you don't like, then? If I guess, will you tell me?"

"You won't guess."

"Dwayne?"

"Did someone tell you?"

"No. Is that it? Did I really guess it on the first try?"

"Someone told you."

"No, I swear."

He shook his head with a smile. "You're just good at everything you do, huh?"

The ice didn't keep my cheeks from blushing.

"It's my father's name and his father's."

"And what about the J?"

"I'm sure you already know that one too."

"I don't," I said.

"Jeremy."

"Dwayne Jeremy. It kind of rolls off the tongue."

He laughed. "Right? It really doesn't. That's why I've gone by DJ forever."

"Well, your secret is safe with me."

He held my eyes for a moment, like I'd said something significant. Had I?

His gaze dropped to the floor, and he changed the subject. "I don't think I've ever seen you as wound up before a race as you were a few minutes ago."

"Just a little distracted." And I thought I'd be less distracted away from everything, but back here I was worried I'd miss the race. "I better get out there."

We walked side by side to the pool. My gaze immediately went to the stands. Not only was Jackson still sitting by my dad, who was laughing, but on his other side was my mom. I thought she'd left after my first two races but she was back in her seat, no phone in sight, full attention on Jackson. They looked like a perfect little family. It was like I'd been transported back twenty years and was getting a glimpse of exactly what it had been like. What they'd lost.

"You okay?"

I was gripping DJ's arm. He might've been the only thing keeping me upright. "I'm fine. Good. Perfect."

Where was Amelia? I needed Amelia. I scanned the deck and saw her sitting on the side, staring at me . . . and

DJ. I dropped his arm. "Thanks for the ice," I said, then made my way to her, weaving through Speedo-clad guys and coaches holding clipboards. When I reached her, I sat down with a sigh.

"I didn't realize your shoulders were bothering you."

"Yeah."

She poked at the ice. "Or did you just need an excuse to see DJ?"

"What? No. I needed to get out of here. Do you see my parents?"

She looked. "What about them?"

"That's Jackson."

"Oh yeah. It is. Weird."

"What if my dad tells him about my brother? The truck?"

She shrugged. "Then you wouldn't have to."

"Don't you think my parents look happy up there?"

"Your parents always look happy."

She wasn't getting it. Not that she should've. I hadn't filled her in on what my dad had said. But seeing her reaction made me think that maybe I was overreacting. Yes, I was overreacting. Especially right now, before a race, before the relay where three other girls would be depending on me to have my head on straight.

"Do you like DJ?"

I ripped my gaze away from my parents. "What?"

"DJ. Do you like him?"

I shook my head. "No. Not at all. You still like him, right?"

"Yes. A lot. And I really don't want to have to compete against you."

"What does that mean?"

"I mean, every boy you give the tiniest amount of attention to falls at your feet."

That was so untrue, I didn't even know where it was coming from. "Like who?"

"DJ."

"He was just icing my shoulders."

"Robert." She pointed to the stands and I looked up and saw that he too was up there, watching the meet. He wasn't here for me. Luke was on the swim team. He was here for Luke.

"He broke up with me, in case you forgot."

"Jackson."

"The guy who is single-handedly trying to drive me crazy?"

"Heath Hall."

My mouth dropped open. "Heath Hall? He's not even real." I took her by the shoulders. "Amelia, if those are your only examples, then I reject your statement. None of those guys are anywhere close to falling at my feet."

I looked her straight in the eyes. "I promise I don't like DJ. He's all yours."

She smiled and hugged me. "I'm sorry. I just get so jealous."

"I know."

She shoved me away with a laugh. "You love me anyway."

"Always."

A whistle blew by the timing table. "Let's get your shoulder pads off. It's time to swim a relay."

Amelia swam the best relay of her life. I swam the worst of mine.

EIGHTEEN

I tried to forget about the awful swim. About the way everyone congratulated me like it wasn't an awful swim. About how Coach didn't even mention it. About how my shoulders hurt so bad that I feared I wouldn't be able to swim for a week. It was over. The season was over. There was nothing I could do about it now, so I wasn't going to dwell on it.

I was also trying to avoid my parents. I didn't need to hear from Mom that she agreed with my dad about Jackson. So I shrugged off an after-swim celebration, claiming exhaustion, and had been holed up in my room ever since.

Now I was showered and dressed, with ten minutes to spare before Amelia picked me up for the Heath Hall event. And even though he wasn't real, as I had stated very confidently to Amelia earlier that day, and even though he was probably already on his way to the bridge, I found myself on the computer again typing out a message.

Good luck tonight.

I was surprised when he quickly replied, Are you going?

Of course.

It's nice to have support when facing fears.

So this was about a fear. He was afraid to bungee jump. **Don't you always? It seems like these things are pretty packed.**

Not always. Sometimes it's something that needs to be done alone.

I wondered what things he had to face alone. **Do you still wear the mask even when nobody is there to watch?**

There's power in the mask.

Like Dumbo's black feather?

Yes, but a lot hotter.

Do you mean temperature wise or looks wise?

You tell me.

Hmm. Not sure I find rubber masks appealing.

Now you're just trying to hurt my feelings.

I smiled. **Is the mask now a part of you?**

He's a part of all of us.

You're a dork.

There was a pause. One that made me regret calling him that.

What happened today? he asked.

I analyzed that question. Was he just asking me about my day? Was he asking about the swim meet? He was there, then? Someone on the swim team? No, him jumping into the pool with the mask on didn't support that. I tried to remember who'd been at the meet but could only remember a few people. Jackson. Robert.

I choked, I responded.

Why?

It was my turn to pause. There were so many reasons. Talking to DJ. Amelia grilling me. My parents. Jackson. My shoulders. I let too much in. I should've kept the headphones on like I had planned. Stared at the pool. Shut it all out. Kept my walls up. I got distracted.

I can't always be perfect.

Before he could respond, Amelia honked her horn out front and I quickly typed, **See you later,** and shut the laptop. On my way out the door I grabbed a sweatshirt. It was supposed to get cold once the sun went down.

★ ★ ★

The bridge was even more crowded than the museum. Partly because people unrelated to the Heath Hall thing were there to jump and support their friends and partly because of Heath Hall. We'd been there awhile and the Heath Hall crowd was getting a little antsy—constantly looking toward the parking lot, their watches, their phones. I tugged on my hood because I was cold.

Amelia hooked her arm in mine and said, "I know you don't do sugar, but I want hot chocolate." We headed toward the concession carts that had become part of the scenery after bungee jumping off the bridge was taken over by Just Jump.

"When are you going to call Robert?" she asked.

"I should probably wait until we see Heath Hall come out. Maybe when he's jumping. That way I can hear his voice and see Heath at the same time."

She stopped, making us both stop. "Oh no. I want kettle corn instead."

"Why?" But right as I said that, I saw why she'd changed her mind. Jackson stood in the hot chocolate line. Irritation surged through me. He was one of the reasons I swam so badly earlier. His need to hang out with my parents had distracted me. I wasn't going to give him the satisfaction of knowing that, though. I swallowed my irritation to prove I could ignore Jackson.

"No, it's fine. You can still get hot chocolate."

"You sure?"

I nodded. "Guess we can mark him off the Who Is Heath Hall list."

"He was never on it."

"He was my top suspect," I said as a joke. He wasn't my top, but he had entered my mind. He seemed like the right personality. The prankster type.

"Hi, Jackson," she said when we arrived in line behind him.

"Amelia. Moore."

"Why do you call me by my first name and Hadley by her last name?" I should've told Amelia we were ignoring him. But her question was one I was curious to know the answer to as well. I'd just assumed he called everyone by their last names, but hearing him greet us together like that made it stand out.

"Because Moore is a last-name kind of girl." Somehow he made even that sound like a joke.

"What does that mean?" I asked. Apparently, I couldn't ignore him.

"I know what he means," Amelia said.

"You do?" I asked.

"In sports they generally refer to people by their last names. And you are the epitome of a sports girl."

I looked back to Jackson to see if Amelia's analysis was right.

"You are that," he said, but that response didn't really confirm her theory.

Amelia seemed to think it did and beamed. "See?"

He reached the front of the line and ordered three hot chocolates. Then he turned around and handed one to Amelia and one to me.

"Thank you, Jackson," Amelia said, wrapping both hands around her cup.

I took the cup, not wanting to be rude. Maybe avoiding sugar didn't matter anyway; the season was over. And even after all my sacrifices, it had ended poorly.

"Technically, Moore, you owe *me*, seeing as how I beat you in that swim competition at Sarah's. But I'm not a sore winner, so this is my prize to you."

Would. Not. React. I raised the cup with a smile of acknowledgment.

We walked toward an open spot, weaving around camping chairs and blankets spread out on the dirt bank running perpendicular to the bridge as if this was some rock concert or fireworks show.

"Maybe we should have another friendly wager tonight." Jackson nodded toward the bridge. "Let you win back some of your pride. Should we see who can jump the farthest?"

Just Jump had set up a measuring pole for the "competitors at heart." The pole was attached to the railing, extending straight out from the bridge, and they kept records of the people with the ten farthest leaps.

Amelia looked up at the leaderboard with his mention of a competition. "Hey, you're number three."

My eyes went to the board as well, and sure enough, J. Holt was in the number three spot, which of course made me want to strap on some gear and go charging off the bridge.

"Is that from tonight?" Amelia asked.

"Last summer. Think you can beat me, Moore?"

This time I was going to ignore the desire. "I would, but you probably cheated."

He gave a small chuckle.

"Why were you hanging out with Hadley's parents today?" Amelia asked.

I shot her a hard look.

"They seem to like me. I can't help that I'm so likable." He met my eyes as if challenging me to contradict him. I couldn't this time. Even though I had avoided my parents so they couldn't tell me that very thing today, I knew it was true—they did like him.

Amelia let out a small yelp. "Look who's here."

I followed her outstretched finger to see DJ standing by a group sitting on a plaid blanket.

"Did you invite him again?" I asked.

"No, I swear. But I better go claim my territory before

Naomi does." She skipped off, leaving me behind with Jackson.

"Isn't that guy like thirty or something?"

"He's eighteen. He graduated last year."

"Oh. I was way off."

A girl stood on the jump platform of the bridge, all strapped in, her ponytail sticking out from beneath the helmet. She stepped up to the edge, then over it, a scream echoing behind her the whole way down.

"It's not very hot," he said.

I paused. "What?"

He nodded toward my drink. "You're not drinking it. I thought maybe you thought it was too hot."

"Oh. No . . ."

"You don't like hot chocolate? Are you more of a hot cider girl?"

"Ew. No. Only people over eighty like hot cider."

He smiled big. "I love hot cider, but I can never find it around here."

"That's because nobody likes it."

He laughed. "You're probably right."

"Have you tried Starbucks?" I suggested.

"They only sell hot apple juice. Not the same thing."

"If you say so."

His attention was drawn to my cup again. "So, seriously, why aren't you drinking it?"

Why didn't I want to tell him? Maybe because people had been making me feel weird about my strict commitment to swimming lately. There was nothing wrong with commitment, sacrifice. "I avoid sugar when I can."

A horrified expression came onto his face. "Why?"

"It helps me swim better."

"Wow" was his only response, and I couldn't tell if it was an impressed wow or a patronizing one.

I gripped the cup a little tighter. The heat seeping into my palms felt good.

"Don't you want to know something about me now?" he asked. When I only lowered my brows, he said, "I found out something about you. Now you ask me something. It's what friends do."

"I found out about your cider preference. That was a friendship deal breaker for me."

He smiled, but I could tell my indifference was really bugging him. He was used to everyone liking him, and I didn't. Was this why he couldn't just walk away from me: He really was determined to make me his friend? To prove he could? I almost laughed out loud at this realization. He *needed* everyone to like him. I could ask him one question about himself. That wouldn't be hard. I stared at him for a moment.

His brown hair was a curly mop on his head. It was

short on the sides and longer on top. Did his dad have curly hair? His mom? Had he ever grown it out long? No, those weren't questions I could really ask, so I continued down to his face. Like I'd noted before, he had green eyes. But he was lucky: instead of having my pale skin, he had an olive undertone to his. His lashes were thick and curled up. Did guys curl their lashes or was that natural? My hand reached into my pocket only to find it empty. I'd left my earphones at home. Not that I was going to put them in right now, but just feeling them in my pocket helped me relax.

His lips were on the thin side and his teeth were very white. I could tell that because he was smiling big right now. "Did you have braces?" I finally decided on.

"Yes, I did."

There. I'd asked him a question. My eyes were on the leaderboard again, seeing his name and the distance he'd jumped. "Why don't you do any sports, *Holt*?" I emphasized his last name with my question. He was obviously athletic. He beat me out at the lake. Sure, he'd cheated, but even if he hadn't, he'd held his own pretty well. And his name occupied space number three on the leaderboard here and had for months now.

"Waste of my talent," he said. "I'd rather do student council."

"What do you do on student council?"

"Not much."

"You could do both student council and sports."

"And sacrifice my C average? I don't think so."

"Do you even try?"

"At what?"

"At anything?"

"Trying sounds like work." With that, he flashed me a smile and walked away.

Amelia joined me a few minutes later. "You managed to shake Jackson? How'd you do that?"

"I think I might have offended him."

"I don't think Jackson gets offended."

Either way, it's what I'd wanted—for him to walk away. Wasn't it?

"You want this?" I asked, holding up my hot chocolate.

"Of course." She snatched the drink from me, and we watched a couple more people jump off the platform.

"Where is DJ?" I asked.

"He's going to come join us in a minute. He's right there."

I looked where she'd indicated and didn't see him anywhere. "Where?"

She narrowed her eyes. "Well, he was. He'll be right

back or I will hunt him down."

"Does he know what he's gotten himself into with you?"

She wiggled her eyebrows. "He will soon enough."

A new person stepped up to the jumping platform. "It's him," I said.

"You see DJ?"

"No, Heath Hall." I grabbed Amelia by the arm and worked my way forward, through onlookers now focused on him, until we were to the front where he could see me. For whatever reason, I wanted him to know I was here.

A low murmur rippled through the crowd. He turned, a harness on, his mask firmly in place. I thought back to our chat earlier about fear and wondered if he was scared right now. I stood on my tiptoes to try and see him better. His gaze went over the crowd. I waited for it to stop on me. It didn't. He held his arms out to the sides.

"Suck it, fear!" he said, and then fell backward.

Amelia laughed.

My lip curled. "'Suck it, fear'? That was his big speech? 'Suck it'?"

She laughed again. "It was awesome."

I was disappointed and couldn't figure out why. I

didn't need him to acknowledge me in any way. This wasn't about me. He obviously didn't need my help facing his fear.

Amelia grabbed my arm. "Call Robert!"

"Oh! Right!" I whipped out my phone and quickly dialed as Heath Hall dangled on the end of the rope. It rang and rang until finally it spit me out into his voice mail.

"Anything?" Amelia asked when I hung up.

"He didn't answer."

"So technically . . ." She tilted her head toward the bridge.

"I guess."

"'Suck it, fear,'" Amelia said. "That's going to be my go-to line from now on when I'm scared to do something."

"Please, no."

"'Suck it, fear,'" she said again through a laugh. "Come on, let's go find DJ."

She turned on her heel and walked away. I stayed two beats longer and watched Heath Hall being lowered into the waiting boat below, not wanting to admit to myself that of the words he uttered before jumping, two were words Robert had used all the time.

NINETEEN

The next week went by slowly. I had taken a step back from the whole Heath Hall thing. I hadn't even checked my messages all week. The bungee jumping night left me with a bad taste in my mouth. He had seemed more thoughtful when we chatted online. Even though I hadn't divulged too much to him, there was something about the chats that made me think. That made me analyze myself. He knew how to ask the right questions. Which was very un-Robert-like. But even if he wasn't Robert, I was beginning to wonder if he chatted with everyone online. If that was another part of his need for attention. Maybe I didn't know him in real life, after all.

So when Amelia had told me that he'd given the information online this week about where he'd be, I wasn't even upset that I'd have to miss it due to the charity dinner. Amelia was. Very upset. That's why she was calling me again one hour before I had to leave for the dinner.

"What if tonight is the night he chooses to unmask himself and swear the room to whatever secrecy pact they seem to have? What if we miss it because you're at your brother's thing and I'm at the stupid swim awards with my parents and brother? Maybe I can get out of it. What if I came up with a really good excuse? One of us needs to be there to see him take off the mask tonight."

"He's not going to take off the mask," I said, trying to curl my hair one-handed. It wasn't a task I was fluent in two-handed, so it was going badly.

"He might. Maybe he'll do it just to make us mad when he sees we aren't there."

"I don't think he'll notice we're not there. I don't think he cares that much about us," I said, admitting out loud the thing I'd been feeling all week.

"Ugh. I don't feel good."

"You don't?" Maybe Amelia was feeling the same disappointment I was.

"Was that convincing? Would that convince Coach if I called him?"

"Do you want to swim next year?"

She sighed. "Fine. I'm going, but it's going to be so boring without you."

I wished I could go. It wasn't too late to go. I put down the curling iron. It was way too late.

"Okay, I gotta go find my cutest outfit for DJ."

"You mean for the awards ceremony."

"Sure. That's what I meant."

We hung up, and I finished curling my hair. My hair was usually pulled back into a messy bun or ponytail, so it took me awhile to analyze if it actually looked good because it seemed so foreign at first. I wore the dress I wore to the museum like my mom had suggested. The dress wasn't very comfortable. I had only bought it because Amelia insisted, so why was I wearing it again? Because my mom wanted me to. I went to my closet and pulled out a different dress that I changed into. I knew this was my passive-aggressive way of rebelling against tonight. I needed to find the courage now to do something a little less subtle. To actually say out loud to my parents that I was only doing this tonight for them and I wished Mom would support me more in *my* events.

I could say that. I would say that.

I shook my head and tried to concentrate on the speaker now up at the podium at the charity dinner. I felt guilty for letting my mind wander. My mom eyed my plate, which was still more than half full of food: chicken, rice, and vegetables. I wasn't hungry. Which was rare because of how much I swam. But now that the season was over, I hadn't swum all week. Maybe that was why I felt off. I thought the break would help my shoulders but they were stiffer than ever.

When the speaker finished to a round of applause, the lights dimmed and a video came up on the big screen. It was a different video every year. My mom always helped put it together. It usually followed the story of a local family and their struggles with the illness, then it finished with a slideshow of the faces in the community of those we'd lost over the years. Eric's face was up there every year, a different picture each time. I watched the faces flash on and off the screen. Some were getting as familiar to me as my own brother's.

"There he is," my dad said in a soft voice when Eric's picture came up. My dad smiled; my mom's eyes glistened with tears. Me, nothing. No, actually, there was irritation. Instead of the pleasant feeling of fondness I'd had every other year, this year my dad had put a personality to my brother. Jackson's personality. So seeing his smile up there made me imagine all the childish pranks he'd probably played on his friends and unsuspecting people. How much he needed people to like him. It made me think of how much my parents seemed to love that personality and not the hardworking one that I had.

My mom gave me a soft smile. "So glad you came tonight."

Now was definitely not the time to say that I wished I could've gone to the awards banquet. I hadn't even needed them to go with me.

Wait. They hadn't offered that. . . . They hadn't offered to go with me.

They only said it was my choice which one I wanted to go to. How come I hadn't realized that before this moment? I looked down at my hands resting in my lap.

Mom reached over and squeezed my hand. She probably thought I was sad about the video. I probably should've been sad about the video. About my brother. Crap. Here I was again having a one-track mind. Only thinking about something related to swimming. I'd made the choice to be here; now I needed to be all here.

I refocused my energy up front, where a speaker was now talking about how important donations were and where the money from these donations went.

After the ceremony our table was bombarded with people. My mom was somewhat famous in this little community. People loved her. Last year she had gotten some award for how much money she had helped raise for the cause over the years.

A hand grabbed mine and shook it. I met the eyes of a kind older gentleman. "You must be so proud of your mother," he said.

"Always." And that was true.

"I'm sorry for your loss."

It took me too long to realize he was talking about my brother. "Right. Thank you," I replied.

"What's going on with you tonight?" Mom whispered when he walked away.

"I don't know. A lot on my mind, I guess."

She put her arm around my shoulders. "Can you be present tonight? It's important. Today's Eric's day."

Every day seemed to be Eric's day. "I'm trying."

"Thank you."

"We can get Froyo after this, right?" Dad asked, coming up behind us.

"Don't call it that," Mom and I said at the same time.

He laughed. "It's so much easier, though."

When my mom turned to greet more people, Dad nudged my shoulder with his. "You okay, kid?"

"Yes, I think. Tired. You?"

"Hungry. That chicken was dry. I think I'm going to suggest a different menu for next year. I have some pull with one of the organizers." He winked at me.

"Next year . . ." A future of endless charity events stretched out before me. If I couldn't get out of it this year with a legitimate excuse, it was hopeless.

I was tired when I got home, so I shouldn't have turned on my laptop. I should've just gone to sleep. But curiosity got the better of me and I clicked on pictures from the Heath Hall event we'd missed tonight—a night trek through some orchard. My eyes drifted to the envelope icon in the corner. It showed eight notifications. I clicked on it. There were a couple from Amelia, but I went straight to the ones from Heath Hall. The first one thanked me for being at the bungee jumping night. I rolled my eyes. He didn't seem to care at all when I was there.

The next few asked how I was. Finally, the last one asked where I'd been. So he did notice when I wasn't around.

I sent him a message. **Has that stupid mask ever failed you?**

After I hit Send, I realized the question came off a bit cranky. I wasn't in the best mood. I probably shouldn't have been sending him messages at all when I felt this way toward him, toward my parents.

How so? he responded.

I could've just dropped it, but I really did want to

know. Have you ever set out to face a fear or reveal a truth or whatever it is you do and failed? Has your fear ever beat you?

Yes.

That was all he said. He didn't expand or explain. But even just that simple confession calmed me a bit. I felt like I'd failed tonight. I wanted to tell my parents a truth and I let the truth be buried with their expectations.

What about you?

Every time. My finger hovered over the Send button, and I almost didn't push it but realized how ironic that would be if, once again, I couldn't admit a truth because of fear. So I hit Send and waited.

A few moments later this message came back. You just have to put shoes on and step on them.

What kind of unhelpful metaphor was that? I stared at the words, feeling stupid I had confided in him if that was his advice, when another message popped up.

Spiders, right? That's what you said you were afraid of.

I laughed. That's right. I had told him the only fear I had was of spiders and now he was calling me on my BS. You're right. How come I didn't think of that all this time? I just need bigger shoes. Thanks.

You're welcome. Some call me the master advice giver.

Really? Who calls you that?

My dog, mostly. Well, he would if he could talk. We have this mental-telepathy thing going on. I know what he thinks.

Wow. You have mental conversations with dogs. I'm not sure that's something you should admit to.

Hey, I've told you before. I can admit anything I want behind the anonymity of the mask.

True.

So I know your spiders confession wasn't a confession at all. What is it you're really afraid of?

I sighed. Was it time to tell him something real? He hadn't told anybody about our conversations so far. At least nobody had called me out on chatting with the fake Heath Hall. So I found myself typing some honesty. **I'm not even sure, but I know I can never tell my parents what I'm thinking if what I am thinking will be something I know they don't want to hear. Actually, I can't tell anyone what I'm thinking if I know they don't want to hear it.**

How do you know they don't want to hear it?

Because people only want to hear their own thoughts reflected back at them.

And what do you think will happen if they hear something they don't like?

I don't know.

So you fear unknown reactions?

Maybe. What *was* I so afraid of? That my parents would yell at me? It's not like I'd never been yelled at before. **I don't know.** And admitting that was hard to this guy who seemed to not only know exactly what he feared but to embrace those fears and talk about them with everybody.

It seems your mask helps other people reveal their truths too, I typed.

Yes, it does.

Now if only I could reveal mine to the right people, not the anonymous ones.

TWENTY

The classroom phone rang midlecture and Mr. Kingston walked to the wall and picked it up. He met my eyes as he talked. He nodded at me like I should know what was being said on the other end. When he hung up, he said, "Hadley, please gather your things and meet your coach in his office."

I had only one coach, but I still said, "Coach Phillips?"

"Yes."

As I shut my binder and stuffed it into my backpack, my heart picked up speed. I'd missed the awards banquet.

Was this the time where I learned the consequences of that? Was he going to tell me I couldn't swim next year? Take away a race from me? Lecture me about my irresponsibility? I had a good relationship with Coach but he was a coach—he expected a lot from us. I pushed myself to standing and slowly walked to the door.

Maybe this wasn't even about the banquet at all. Maybe this was about how awful I'd swum in the relay. He was finally going to talk to me about that. Tell me how disappointed he'd been. Or maybe he knew how much my shoulders had been bugging me. He was going to tell me I shouldn't be swimming at all.

I quickly retrieved my earbuds out of my pocket and turned on my music. It helped drown out my thoughts but didn't seem to calm my heart.

When I finally made it to his office, I was convinced I was going to die of a heart attack. I knocked on the glass. He looked up from his desk and waved me in. His face was stone, like always, giving away nothing.

He pointed to the chair in front of his desk.

I didn't want to sit. If I sat, he would talk.

I sat. Coach was tall, really tall. And sitting in front of him like this made him seem even taller.

He gestured to his ears.

Oh. My music.

I yanked on the cord and the earbuds fell to my lap,

leaving a ringing buzz in their place.

"Good afternoon," he said. "I haven't seen you out at the pool lately."

"I've been busy. I'm starting club swim next week, though. I'm committed."

He smiled. "I know." He turned on his spinning chair to the cabinet behind him and picked up a padded orange envelope, bringing it back to the desk between us. "That's what I wanted to talk to you about."

"I know I can be annoying. I'll work on that."

"Hadley. Do you think you're in trouble?"

"I don't know."

He laughed. "You're not in trouble. Relax."

He said it, but I couldn't force myself to do it. He opened the envelope and pulled out a plaque. The outline of a swimmer was etched into the wood and below the swimmer was a gold square. Something was etched there as well but I couldn't make it out. He slid the plaque across the desk until it rested in front of me.

"Congratulations."

"What is it?"

"I know you couldn't make it to the awards banquet because of the event for your brother, so you get it today."

"I won an award? For what?"

"For being annoying," he said.

"What?"

"A joke. It's for being my most dedicated swimmer on the team. You ready to swim four races next year?"

"Really?"

"Really."

My heart wasn't going to survive the workout I was putting it through today. "Thank you!"

"Thank *you*. I mean it. Like I told the team at the ceremony the other night, you are what commitment looks like. I'm proud of you. I wish you could've been there to get recognized in front of everyone, but I understand."

"Amelia didn't tell me about this."

"I asked the team not to tell you. I wanted to be the first."

I gripped the plaque, staring at the words etched into the gold: *Coach's Award. Dedication and Commitment. Hadley Moore.* "I wish my mom knew I was winning an award. Then we would've been there for sure."

"I talked to your mom."

"I know, but she just thought it was a team requirement and I told her that usually only seniors win the awards."

He took off his baseball cap and ran his hand back and forth over his short hair, then replaced the cap. He seemed to decide against whatever he had been thinking about saying and handed me the now-empty envelope. "Congratulations."

That's when I realized what he wasn't saying. "You told her."

"Maybe she didn't understand. I should've explained it better."

"You told her about this award? That I was winning it?" He nodded.

I started to make excuses for my mom. "It's tradition . . . this thing for my brother. . . ." I trailed off when I saw the pity in his eyes. "Never mind." I stood so fast that the chair fell over. I scrambled to pick it up, dropping the envelope. It slid beneath the chair I'd just righted. I grabbed it and made for the door. "Thanks for this."

"Hadley—" he said, but I had already left. The shutting door cut off however he was going to finish that sentence.

My eyes stung. I just needed to get out of there, I thought as I walked as quickly as I could away from the office, trying to figure out where I could go. I made it out of the gym and around one corner before I slammed into Jackson. The award, the envelope, and I went flying backward. The clatter of metal bouncing along cement had me searching the ground where I had landed.

"Are you everywhere?" I growled.

"Moore. I'm sorry." He held out his hand to help me up.

I picked up the plaque and saw the gold plate that spelled out the distinction was missing. It sat by Jackson's foot. He bent over and picked it up.

"Nice," he said, after reading it. "Congrats."

I ripped it from his hand, scooped up the envelope where it had landed, and shoved the two now separate pieces of my award inside. Then I left. Of course he followed me.

"I'm trying to understand you, Moore."

"Stop."

"You hate me."

"Hate is a strong word."

He laughed. "Wow. I thought you'd deny it, but that was definitely not a denial. That was probably the furthest thing from a denial I've ever heard. Why don't you like me?"

"Why do you care?" I asked quite suddenly.

He shrugged like he really didn't.

My heart was pumping and my head was spinning and I just wanted Jackson out of my face. "You want to know why, Jackson? Why people like me don't like people like you?"

"Yes, actually."

"Because you're a goof-off. You do nothing. Life is a joke to you. You just sail through it. All you think about is yourself and what you need to do to make people look at you. I work hard. Every day. And I try my best and I push myself in everything I do so they'll notice me and do you know who still gets all the attention? Who everybody talks about? Who everyone is still more proud of and happier with and can't forget about? Who everybody loves the most? You, Eric." I stopped and swallowed hard. "I mean, Jackson. You . . ."

He had gone silent. I swiped at the tears that were trailing down my face, mad that I hadn't been able to hold them back for a few more minutes. Then I turned and fled. I didn't make it far before I couldn't see through the blurriness. Worried I was going to run into a wall, I turned a corner and pressed my back against the building. If I had thought now was the time Jackson would grow up and leave me alone, I was mistaken.

He rounded the corner a few seconds after me.

"Please don't," I said.

For once he looked serious, somber. "I promise I'll leave if you want me to, but is there anything I can do? Do you want me to go get Amelia? Or call your parents?"

I shook my head no.

"Could you use someone to cry on? I think I'm good at that. I wore an extra absorbent sweater today." He opened his arms like he expected me to melt into them. When I didn't, he said, "How about a different offer, then?" He pulled his car keys out of his pocket. "The bell is about to ring and these halls are going to fill with people. My car, you remember it, the classic, is a great place to cry. I know it doesn't have music, but it does have doors that can close people out. Even me if you want. Or I can drive you to a completely new location. I won't even talk."

My tears started anew. Why was he choosing now to be thoughtful? I had just yelled mean, awful things at him, and he stood there offering me salvation. I nodded.

"Yes?"

"Please."

He held out his hand like a question and I took it. I could still hardly see, so I was glad he was guiding me. Like he'd warned, the bell rang. He brought me closer and put his arm around me. I hid my face against his shoulder, hoping nobody would know it was me. We made it to the parking lot without anyone calling out to me. I hoped that was a good sign. He unlocked the door to his car with his weird two-lefts-and-one-right-turning method and opened it wide. I dropped all my stuff onto the passenger-side floor and practically dived inside. He shut the door behind me. I laid my head on the seat and let it all out.

TWENTY-ONE

Like Jackson promised, he didn't say a word. He was quiet as he started the car and drove. I didn't sit up to see where he was driving us, but I was glad he was leaving the school. Eventually he parked and shut off the car. He still hadn't said anything. I wondered if this was a record for him.

The seat smelled a little of gas or grease or something— that old-car smell. I sat up, wiped my cheeks with my sleeve, and peered out the front window. He'd driven us to Lookout Point above the lake. My lake. This wasn't the side of the lake I swam on. This was the side where everyone at school went to drink or make out. I turned my gaze to him and he held up his hands.

"It was the first quiet place I could think of."

"You come here a lot?"

He laughed. "Yes." Then, after a minute of silence added, "But not in the way you're thinking. I like to walk. It helps me think. I like nature."

It really was beautiful. The trees were in full spring green. Wildflowers covered the ground where the cars hadn't driven. And the lake was a dark sheet of glass below us. I pulled my sleeves over my hands and used them again to wipe beneath my eyes, sure they were black with mascara.

"Do you want to talk about it?" he asked.

"I'm sorry for what I said about you."

"Don't apologize for how you feel."

"I'm sure you can guess that it's not really about you."

He nodded slowly. "Who's Eric?"

"My brother."

"So your brother is a screwup like me and he gets all the attention for it?"

"You're not a screwup."

"I didn't realize you had a brother."

Did I want to tell him? I knew it would clear up some of the bad feelings he might have over what I'd said. But it would turn those feelings into pity and I wasn't ready for that. Not yet. "I kind of live in his shadow and have been trying to get out of it for years."

"Hence the swimming for hours on end?"

"I like to swim."

"I know. But . . ."

"Yes, I always have to be better and do more. I don't know. . . . I guess I thought if I did the most and did it the best maybe I could make them . . . see me." I had been competing with my dead brother. No wonder why I hadn't been crying at his ceremonies. I had started seeing him as the enemy, the competition. Was I seriously just now realizing my motivations for how hard I pushed myself? And in front of Jackson Holt? That was my fear, wasn't it? The one I couldn't articulate to Heath Hall the other night. The reason I feared expressing my frustrations to my parents. I feared that if I told my parents how I really felt, they would admit that there was no competition. They would admit that Eric had already won. And if they admitted it, then I couldn't keep pretending everything was fine. I couldn't talk myself out of that truth.

I turned toward the window and wiped at a fresh set of tears that silently slipped down my cheeks. It took a few deep breaths for me to regain my control and turn back again.

Jackson pointed to the padded envelope on the floor.

"So you won an award for your parents?"

I laughed, then sniffled. "Yes! And do you want to know the worst part about it? It didn't matter. They didn't want to go to the awards ceremony. They still chose him."

He seemed to analyze my comment. "Was it a choice between an event for him and one for you?"

I let out a humorless laugh. "Yes, actually, it was."

"But that's not fair. I mean, that would be hard for a parent to have to choose between their kids. You must've wanted to support him too because you obviously missed your own awards ceremony if you were just getting that award today."

"I did miss my awards ceremony. For his charity banquet."

"I'm sure he appreciated it."

"He didn't."

"Unless he told you that he didn't, you can't just assume—"

"He's dead."

He cussed under his breath, then his eyebrows shot up. "Well, technically you still can't assume he didn't appreciate it."

I laughed.

"Now you laugh at me?"

"I already cried enough, right?"

"I'm sorry. When did he . . ."

"Die?"

"Yes."

"Eighteen years ago."

"So . . ."

"I didn't know him. He died of cancer before I was born. That truck on our lawn? That's his truck. It's been there for eighteen years." I put my head back against the seat. "If that truck won an award the same night I did, they would go to its ceremony over mine because it belonged to my brother."

"But what if the truck won an award the same night as the charity dinner?" He was trying to make me laugh again. It kind of worked.

"The truck would be out of luck."

"And the truck would have a right to be pissed."

I laughed louder this time. "Really? In this fake scenario you've presented, you think my parents should pick the truck's award ceremony over my brother's charity dinner?"

"Well, no, but in my head that was a much better metaphor where I was making you the truck and telling you that you have a right to be pissed."

I smiled. "Yeah, I got that."

He wasn't smiling anymore. "Did you? Because, Moore . . ." He met my eyes. "You have a right to be pissed."

"I am." I pressed my palms to my eyes, even though I knew that was just going to make a bigger mess of my mascara. "But mostly I'm just sad."

I brought my knees up on the seat with me and hugged them against my chest, resting my forehead on them while more tears fell. This was so embarrassing. "You have to promise me this doesn't leave your car."

"Nobody would believe me anyway."

"What's that supposed to mean?"

"Moore. Tough, competitive, stoic swim star. You're kind of known for walking through the halls in the zone. Your headphones in. Your game face on. Your veins pumping chlorine."

"Okay, I get it." I had been shutting out my problems, and apparently people, for years, trying not to think about how I felt second-best in my home.

Jackson moved next to me and put his arm around my shoulders. Because of my compact position, I fell against him. I thought about pushing away but I was already there and it felt nice, so instead, I turned my upper body toward his, wrapped my arms around his torso, and didn't try to stop the tears.

His hands went to my back, where they softly ran up and down. Soon they were the only thing I felt, his hands, sending tingles along my spine. I had to remind myself four times that he was still annoying. Very, very annoying. This changed nothing.

He cleared his throat, and as if to prove me right, said, "It's kind of nice to know you have weaknesses like the rest of us. I mean, your problems aren't as bad as most people's but you do actually cry over them."

I let out a single laugh and shoved away from him. "You know, you're really cute when you keep your mouth shut."

His half smile, the one he wore a lot, came onto his face. "You think I'm cute?"

"No, because you can never keep your mouth shut."

"Fair enough."

He was cute, getting cuter by the second, it seemed.

"So does this mean we're friends now?" he asked.

"Until I see you making a fool of yourself at school again."

"So until tomorrow, then?"

I nodded. "Exactly."

We stared out the windshield together toward the lake below.

"I wish I were better at advice," he said. "I've been

trying to think of something cool or comforting to say for the last half an hour and all I can come up with are stupid jokes."

"Jokes? I'm surprised. That doesn't sound like you."

"Yeah, I know."

"I have some advice for you," I said.

"Oh yeah?"

"Yes. Run away from the mess that I am right now. Nobody needs all this drama in their lives." I flipped down the visor, looking for a mirror but there wasn't one.

"Huh. You're not very good at advice either, it sounds like. But I can't even come up with bad advice right now."

I stretched toward the rearview mirror instead and worked at the mascara beneath my eyes. "It's okay. There's really nothing to say. I need to get over this weird competition I have with my brother. It's not like I can confront him. And I should talk to my parents about how I feel. It's not that I think they don't love me or anything. I know they do. Maybe they just don't realize how what they do makes me feel sometimes."

"Your parents seem really cool. They both couldn't stop bragging about you. I mean, neither of them mentioned your brother once at the swim meet the other day. That has to count for something."

I leaned back against the seat. "Did you let them talk?"

He laughed.

"You're right, my parents are cool. But we all live in the past."

"So are you going to talk to them?"

"I'm scared."

"Of what?"

"I'm scared that even if I talk to them about how I feel, they'll still choose him."

"You need to talk to them. You have to give them the opportunity to prove you wrong."

I closed my eyes and smiled. "And you said you were bad at advice."

His hand closed over mine and he twined our fingers together. "I'm even worse at taking it."

TWENTY-TWO

It was two days later and I swore I could still feel the pressure of Jackson's fingers between mine. He had held my hand in the car that day until I was ready to leave. He'd then driven me home, not once asking if I wanted to go back to school. And that made it seem perfectly acceptable that I didn't.

When we'd arrived at my place, he gave my brother's truck a good long stare, very unlike the reaction he'd had the first time he'd seen it. Then he punched my shoulder, like we were pals, and I got out and walked away a little confused as to what now existed between us. I was still confused. That day he'd rescued me I wasn't myself. I was emotional and vulnerable and wasn't thinking straight. I shouldn't have told him half the things I did.

So why did I keep getting this weird sensation in my hand, like I was missing an appendage or something? Like he'd held my hand every day for a year? It had been once. And I hadn't talked to him since.

I stared at the truck on my lawn now as I waited for Amelia to pick me up for school. It was so unassuming. No one looking at it would think it could be the bane of my existence.

Amelia pulled up and waved. "Hey," she said. "Why'd you want me to come early?"

"Can we run by this café about ten minutes out of our way?"

"There's a coffee shop on the way to school if you need a fix. I thought you didn't drink coffee. It messes with your swimming."

"I don't. I'm getting something for someone else."

"Okay, Ms. Cryptic. Who?"

"Drive, we'll talk."

"So I'm confused," Amelia said after I explained to her what I was doing and why I was doing it. We'd pulled into the parking lot of Norman's, but she hadn't let me get out of the car. "Do you *like* Jackson?"

"No, I'm just grateful he saved me the other day." I had downplayed just how much, leaving out the tears and the drama.

"Did you end up talking to your parents about the award?"

"No. I shoved it under my bed and am waiting for the right time."

She turned off the ignition, finally taking in the little shop in front of us. It was a tiny place with peeling paint and dirty windows. "Are we going to die here?"

I got out of the car. "We'll be fine."

After placing my order with the woman behind the counter, I picked up a Sharpie she had in a jar next to the register. "Can I borrow this?"

"Sure, honey." She filled a cup with the amber liquid, put a lid on, and handed it to me. "You know we're the only place around here that carries cider outside of the Christmas season."

"Believe me, I know." On the side of the cup, with the blue Sharpie, I wrote, *Now we're even.*

I figured Jackson was on my mind so much because I was grateful for what he'd done for me. If I sort of paid him back with a kindness, maybe it would help me stop dwelling on it.

Amelia stood in the doorway as if ready to make a

quick exit if necessary. She eyed a bearded man at the far table.

"Do you want anything?" I asked.

"No, I'm good."

I replaced the Sharpie in the jar and we returned to the car.

"What does Jackson have first period?" I asked.

"I'm not sure. Here, I'll find out." She typed something into her phone, then started the engine and backed out of the parking lot.

"Who did you ask?"

"Social media. It knows all."

"You asked the internet world what Jackson has first period?"

"Yes. If he doesn't answer, someone else will."

She was right. By the time we got to school, several people had answered her post. "Peer Counseling, C building."

"Peer Counseling?"

"That's what they said. Four different people."

"And he claimed he was horrible at advice."

"Do you know anyone who actually goes and gets counseled by their peers? I think they just sit around watching movies and stuff."

I honestly didn't know. "Thanks for driving me."

"You're welcome." She headed toward her first class and I headed for Jackson's.

It was still prebell, so I didn't expect him to be in class, but I looked anyway. He sat at a long table in the back, gaze on his phone. There were only a few other people in the room and no teacher yet. I opened the door and went to his table.

"Hey," I said, setting the drink in front of him.

He looked up and surprise lit his face. "Hey. Are you lost?"

"That's for you." I pushed the drink closer. "See you later."

"Moore," he called after me.

I turned around and walked backward a few steps.

"What's it for?"

"Don't ask questions, Holt. Just drink it."

He smiled. He had a nice smile, even though it always looked like it knew a secret.

I happened to catch another guy's eyes as I walked out of the classroom, and he looked just as surprised as Jackson. I glared at him until he looked away. What was the big deal? It was just a drink.

At lunch, as I headed to find Amelia, Jackson fell in step beside me and plucked out one of my earbuds. "We are definitely not even."

I took out the other one and turned off my music. "Why not?"

"Because I just bought you hot chocolate in a line I was already standing in. And you didn't even drink it. You bought me cider. Where did you even find cider around here?"

"It wasn't payback for the hot chocolate. It was payback for the whole me-ruining-your-sweater-with-my-mascara thing."

"Oh, that. Then we're still not even. This beyond pays off the hot chocolate, but as far as the other thing goes, you have to comfort me through an emotional breakdown if you want to be out of debt for that."

"You think you comforted me?"

"Yes. I was very good at it too, so don't try to deny it."

I laughed a little. "You were." Too good.

He lightly punched my shoulder again. I wished he'd stop doing that. "So it's a deal, Moore. I'll find you when I feel the tears coming."

"I'll make sure I'm wearing an absorbent sweater."

He left without another word. I thought about asking him where he was going but stopped myself. Why was it that, when I didn't want him around, he overstayed his welcome and now he was under-staying it?

TWENTY-THREE

I couldn't believe how long it had been since I swam. Eleven days. When had I ever let a busy schedule keep me from swimming before? My entire body sighed a breath of relief as I dived into the water. Muscles that I didn't know were tight relaxed as I began my strokes.

I wasn't sure how much time had passed—it felt like minutes but it could've been hours—before I stopped to rest against the wall. I watched as the water dripped off my arms and pooled onto the cement. A shadow falling over that puddle of water made me look up. I reached to the clip on my swimsuit strap and turned off my music.

★ ★ ★

"Is this from you?" DJ asked, holding up a dollar bill I had penned the words *thank you* on. This was a week of paying back debts.

"Yes. I said I'd give you a dollar if you told Coach I couldn't make the awards ceremony and you did. So there's your dollar."

He shook his head as he laughed. "You don't owe me anything. I didn't really tell Coach anything except that you wanted to talk to him. Your mom had called that same day too, so I passed on both messages." He sat on the ground and set the dollar bill on a dry patch of cement in front of me.

"My mom called *him*? I thought he called her." So much for letting me make my own choice there. She seemed to have made it for me. I couldn't complain. I'd let her.

"Yes, I talked to her. She seems nice."

"She is." That was the problem with my problems. My parents were both nice. It would've been so much easier to tell them off if they were mean.

"Remember that day you ran into me and I dropped all the papers and you saw your name on one?" he asked.

"Yes." That was the day he told me I was too persistent. How could I forget?

"That's what it was about—the award you were winning. Coach had started writing notes about what he was going to include in his speech. Talking about how you never gave up on the butterfly was one of those notes. Sorry I couldn't tell you."

Oh. That made sense. No wonder it seemed like he had been trying to hide something. That made me feel a lot better. "It's okay. You working today?"

"Work makes it sound like I get paid."

"You don't get paid?"

"You didn't know that?"

"I didn't. So why are you always here?"

"I help out the coaches. I want to study sports medicine. I figure it will look good on my graduate application if I have some experience."

"I'm sure it will. So then you're not-working tonight?"

"Yes, getting things ready for track finals tomorrow." He ran a hand through his curls.

"You not-work too much."

"I like to keep busy. The only one that misses me at home is my dog."

"You have a dog?"

"I do."

"Cute. I always wanted a dog, but my mom says they're way too much work."

He nodded. "They are."

A random thought came into my mind. "Do you talk to yours?"

"My dog?"

"Yes." I couldn't read his expression.

"Doesn't everybody?"

I was being stupid. DJ was definitely not Heath Hall. He wasn't even in high school. "Do you know what time it is?"

"After six."

I squeezed my eyes shut. It was late. I'd told my mom I'd be home for dinner.

"You lost track of time again?"

I smiled. "What makes you think that?"

He pointed to my phone sitting on the cement. "You should do a timed playlist. When it's over, you'll know it's time to get out."

"You, DJ, are the smartest man in the world."

His dark skin darkened with a blush, and he messed with his glasses.

I pushed myself out of the pool. When he jumped back, I realized he didn't want to get wet. Being a swimmer, I'd seen that evasion move a lot. I was tempted to hug him, like I was tempted to do with everyone who reacted that way. I stopped myself, though. He and Amelia were . . . something. Instead, I shook my head and sent a spray of water at him.

"Hey!" He laughed and pulled his sweater away from his chest with two fingers.

The dollar bill now sat on the cement between us and we both stared at it.

"I can't take that," he said.

"It'll bring someone luck." I grabbed my towel and wrapped it around me.

"I thought that was a penny."

"Then a dollar should be one hundred times luckier, right?" I said.

"It's hard for me to leave money on the ground. I feel like it's me telling the universe that I don't need any more."

I smiled, and as I walked away said, "Then you better pick it up. Maybe you'll get lucky." Did I really just say that to the guy Amelia liked? I hadn't meant for it to sound so flirty. Maybe it hadn't. I needed to stop.

Five minutes before the bell rang the next morning, I walked into class to find Jackson sitting at my desk. "You have information," he said when I stood beside him, waiting for him to move. "And I need it."

"You need my notes for algebra? I have horrible handwriting, but they're yours if you want them."

"No, I don't need your notes for algebra. What do I look like, a slacker?"

I tilted my head and evaluated him. He had on a red polo shirt and his hair was combed for once . . . or at least the curls were a bit more tamed. He actually looked like he was ready to deliver a speech.

"Fine. I already know you think I'm a slacker, but that's not the information I need."

"Well, spit it out, Holt. The bell is about to ring, and Mr. Kingston does not like your style of humor."

"He belongs to your Jack-haters club?"

"Membership information is confidential."

His eyes twinkled with a smile that didn't reach his lips. "Cider. Where did you get it?"

I laughed under my breath. "That's the information you want? Well, you're out of luck. That's a secret I'm taking to the grave. Now out of my chair." For some reason, I didn't want to tell him about the seedy shop just outside of town. It was like I had some sort of leverage over him and I was hanging on to that.

He stood, then kind of whined the words, "Why? You don't even like cider."

"Because now I own you."

It had been a joke, but the way he raised his eyebrows made me blush.

I shoved him and said, "Oh, stop. If you can joke around, so can I."

"People expect it from me. Things like that from you sound like an invitation."

I blushed even more.

"See?" he said. "I can deliver a joke." He leaned close, then said, "You will tell me where to find that cider eventually."

When he left, I looked around and realized practically everybody was in their seats and staring at me. I quickly sat down. Kendra, the girl who sat next to me said, "When did you two get together?"

"We're not together."

"That was a lot of flirting."

"Jackson is like that with everyone."

"I wasn't talking about Jackson."

Right. She was talking about my behavior, not his. That shut me up.

TWENTY-FOUR

Amelia sat at our normal lunch table with a stack of papers.

"Are you doing homework?"

"Our homework, yes."

"We have homework?"

"Don't we? Don't you still want to know who Heath Hall is? We haven't talked about it in a while."

"Did you learn something new?" I still wanted to know. Probably even more so since I'd been talking to him online. I did not want to be blindsided by his identity, caught off guard. But she was right. We hadn't been working on finding out who he was lately.

"I thought we should sit down and compile a list of the evidence we've collected so we can narrow this down."

I glanced around the crowded courtyard. "Should we really talk about it here?"

"Why not? Everybody seems to have theories about who he is. We should just stand up and ask everybody right now if they are Heath Hall." She stood like she was actually going to yell that question across the cafeteria. I pulled on her arm, forcing her to sit back down.

"Evidence," I reminded her.

"Right. Evidence. I've made lists of all the people at both events, cross-checked it with his followers online. I think I've narrowed it down to two suspects."

"Robert?" I asked, wanting her to disagree with me.

"Yes."

My shoulders slumped. "Wait, you said two. Who else?"

"Jackson."

She let the name hang there while I processed it.

"No, that doesn't make sense. Jackson was at Whitestone Bridge talking to us."

"Exactly. But he mysteriously disappeared when the jumping took place."

I thought back to that night. She was right. About five minutes before the jump, Jackson had left and I hadn't seen him the rest of the night. Was Jackson Heath Hall? As I thought about all the conversations we'd had online, and now in real life too, my heart seemed to sing at that suggestion.

"And Robert," Amelia continued. "He claims to know who he is but hasn't been at a single Heath Hall event to support him."

"You're right." That hadn't occurred to me until now.

"I know."

"Is it weird that our final list includes only people we actually know?" I asked.

"No. I definitely think it's someone we know. He's been private messaging you online. I don't think he does that with anyone else. And besides, we didn't really know Jackson before Heath Hall showed up at the school pool. Then all of a sudden we see him everywhere. Maybe he's trying to keep us from discovering the secret. And Robert, well, he's just been too secretive about this whole thing."

"But wait, Jackson's name was on the Just Jump leaderboard, remember? He'd jumped before and did it well. He wouldn't need to face that fear."

"Maybe he somehow rigged that to throw us off his track."

That did sound like something Jackson would do. He was the one who cheated during our race.

As if he knew we were talking about him, Jackson came running by our table, doubled back, then slid in between me and Amelia on the bench seat.

Amelia flipped over the paper of names in front of her and exchanged a confused look with me.

"Do I blend in?" he whispered.

"What?"

"Will Colton notice me here?" His eyes met mine, sparkling with joy. I couldn't help but smile.

I broke his gaze to look around, and just as I was about to ask him what he was talking about, saw Colton, a big football player, barrel into the courtyard.

"What did you do to him?" Amelia asked.

"Milk in a backpack is nowhere near as bad as milk in a gas tank. Wouldn't you agree, Moore?"

I laughed.

"I could totally take him," Jackson said. "But I don't want to embarrass him."

I nudged his leg with mine. "Sure you could."

He nudged me back and left his thigh pressed there against my leg. That small act made my insides flip. He picked up one of my chips, raised it in the air toward Colton, and gave him that sly smile of his before he popped it in his mouth.

Colton narrowed his eyes. "Jackson, you're a dead man."

"You know you deserved it," he called back.

Colton didn't disagree. He just scowled and walked away.

Jackson put an arm around both me and Amelia and brought us into a group hug. "Thanks for the diversion, ladies. You were perfect." With that, he stood and was gone again.

"See, he's everywhere," Amelia said.

I narrowed my eyes and watched him disappear around a building. "You're right. You were also right about something else—he is kind of funny, I've decided."

Her head whipped toward mine. "What?"

"What? You disagree now?"

She shook her head and flipped the paper back over. "Okay, back to the case. You have still been private messaging Heath Hall, right?"

"Yes."

"Is there a way you can use this new intel to figure out which one he is?"

"I think, yes."

She smiled. "And I'll talk to the two guys this week and see what I can do from my end."

"You're going to ask them if they're Heath Hall?"

"No, I've learned my lesson about that. They won't admit it. I'll be more subtle."

"I can take on one of them too. I mean, you don't have

to try to crack both," I said, focusing on a chip in front of me.

She smiled. "Which one, Hadley? Was there one in particular you want to handle?"

"I hate you."

She laughed. "You've totally been Jacksoned."

"I have not."

She smirked. "Okay, you can have Jackson. I'll deal with Robert."

She stacked her loose papers and put them in her backpack. "So what actually happened? I thought Jackson annoyed you."

"He still does sometimes, but he helped me escape school when I needed it and he was really nice about it. That kind of turned things around for us."

"I can see that." She looked at my still-lingering smile. "He seems to lighten you up a bit."

"What's that mean?"

"You know what it means."

She was right. I did know. And I did feel light. As light as air.

TWENTY-FIVE

My renewed motivation in trying to figure out Heath Hall's identity was a nice distraction from the realization I'd had about my brother. The one I wasn't sure how I was going to fix. How could I get over feeling like he was my enemy when he wasn't even alive for me to confront? When he'd done nothing wrong.

I plopped myself in front of my computer that night, ready to set some traps for Heath Hall where he would slip into admitting something. I may have been even more motivated to figure out who Heath Hall was because of the possibility that he could be Jackson.

Did this mean . . . ? Was Amelia right? Was I crushing on him?

Our chats online had been fun and meant something to me. And our interactions in person had been . . . great.

Before I even signed into my private messages, I saw Heath Hall had announced another event for this weekend. He didn't say exactly what would be happening, just an address and time range. That was new.

I moved on to my messages. I had no new ones. That did not disappoint me, I told myself. I analyzed each of the suspects in my mind, trying to decide which trap to lay first before I typed. A thought occurred to me.

Have any fun mental conversations with your dog lately?

Robert had a dog. How had I not thought about that until now? He didn't respond right away. It was only six o'clock. Had Robert's track meet gone late? Jackson. Where would he be at six o'clock at night? Eating dinner with his family, maybe.

I began scrolling back through Heath Hall's wall. The feed went on and on. How long had he been doing this anyway? I clicked on his profile where it showed me when the account was created. I stared at that date for a long time, then subtracted the number in my head three times from the current date to make sure it was right. Five years. This Heath Hall account had existed for five years? How had I not noticed that before? I just assumed it had only been happening for a couple years because that's when I remembered learning about it. But I was in elementary school five years ago. So were Robert and Jackson, for that matter. There was no way either of them would've thought of something this elaborate five years ago.

My computer dinged with a new message.

My dog is mad that I've been so busy. He's sending me death glares right now but refusing to speak.

Busy? Doing what?

You know, scaling buildings, saving lives, being awesome. The usual.

Five years ago? So did that mean it wasn't Robert *or* Jackson? Was he someone a little older? Robert said I knew who Heath Hall was. Had he been lying? Maybe I didn't know him at all. Maybe he was some senior. I didn't know many seniors very well. Mainly the ones on the swim team. I tried to think of each one, match him up with the clues and facts I knew about Heath Hall. Suddenly and with a jolt of fear, I remembered the one person I knew quite well who was actually out of high school.

DJ.

He would've been in the eighth grade when this account was made. And he was a smart guy, a huge reader. He could've thought of something like this at thirteen. Plus, he was a little closer to the guy I'd always imagined Heath Hall was: shy, kept to himself more. This didn't totally confirm it but I was getting a sick feeling in the pit of my stomach. A bit of guilt coursed through me at how I had acted around DJ at the pool the other day. And another worry burrowed its way into my mind as well. Whoever Heath Hall was, I felt a connection with him. What if it turned out to be DJ? What if it turned out to be none of the above? Someone I didn't know at all?

What about you? he asked.

Nope, I don't have a dog to get mad at me.

Are you not an animal fan?

How did Heath Hall always turn everything back to me? After reading through our conversations, I realized there wasn't much he'd said about himself. Just general things. And he was doing it again.

What is going on tomorrow night? Why the vague announcement?

Are you going to come?

I don't know yet.

You should. You missed the last one.

You noticed?

Doesn't everybody notice you?

My fingers froze on the keyboard. Amelia may have claimed I wouldn't know what flirting was if it slapped me in the face, but I knew that was flirting. Had my flirting with DJ in real life encouraged him to flirt with me now?

Did I scare you away? he asked.

No . . . it's just weird because you know me and I don't know you.

You know me.

I know a lot of people.

You soaked me and my sweater the other day.

The blood rushed from my face, leaving it numb. He just told me who he was. I couldn't believe he just told me who he was. He was DJ . . . or Jackson. Was he talking about soaking him with pool water or tears?

Crap.

I was supposed to react now. He knew it was a big deal to tell me, and it was. And now he wanted me to react. But depending on which one of those it was, my reaction would be completely different. I mean, I really wanted it to be Jackson. I liked Jackson and I wanted him to match up with the online conversations I'd had with Heath Hall. But if I was being truthful, the masked version didn't fit the Jackson I'd come to know. Jackson needing to put on a mask to face all of his fears, Jackson telling his fears to suck it, Jackson shaking like a leaf after showing people his painting didn't make sense.

On the other side, the masked Heath Hall fit more

with the DJ I knew in real life. He was vulnerable and shy. He was more the type that would want to hide his face when facing fears, to not draw attention to himself but the fear, as if it were everyone's to own. Plus, the timeline made more sense. And now I'd flirted with him both online and in real life but Amelia had all but claimed him. Which was fine. I wanted her to. I didn't like DJ like that. Sure I enjoyed the conversations we'd had online and I felt comfortable with him as a friend. I put my forehead to my keyboard. It was him and I so didn't want it to be.

My computer dinged. You're disappointed. It wasn't a question.

No, I responded back, but that was all I had the chance to type before there was a knock at my door. I was glad for the interruption. I needed to think.

"Come in."

My mom opened the door and sat down on the edge of my bed. She looked frazzled, upset. For a minute I thought she had discovered my award under my bed and wanted to apologize for missing the ceremony. But then she started talking. "A friend in Las Vegas called. Her co-organizer came down with the flu and had to go to the hospital because she couldn't hold anything down for several days."

I had no idea who or what she was talking about, but

I figured it would all eventually make sense. "I'm sorry. Is there anything we can do?"

"The race is Saturday. As in the day after tomorrow. You know how crazy race days can be, and she just needs some experienced hands there helping things run smoothly."

Now I understood. Mom to the rescue. "So you're going out of town this weekend?"

"I wouldn't because your father has business down south this weekend too, and I hate to leave you alone. But . . ."

"It's fine, Mom. It's two nights. I think I can survive."

"Dad will be home late Saturday night."

"Well, see, it's just one night, then."

She let out a breath of relief. "I figured you'd be fine but I just wanted to make sure. You think you could stay at Amelia's for the weekend? That would make me feel better."

"Sure. That sounds like fun." I actually wasn't sure. Her aunt was still in town, extending her stay like aunts sometimes do. But a weekend alone sounded nice. If my parents weren't here, I didn't have to think about our issues.

My computer dinged and I felt guilty that I hadn't responded better.

My mom glanced at the computer. "Well, thank you.

Be safe this weekend. No wild parties or anything."

I laughed. "Okay."

She tousled my hair, then left the room.

I turned my attention back to the computer, where the new message awaited.

I thought you'd already figured it out on your own.

Was he referring to the conversation about his dog we had out by the pool? He thought I'd figured it out and that's why he told me? I felt sick. How was I supposed to tell him that all my flirting online wasn't directed at him? How could I tell him that when I'd been flirting in real life too? I couldn't tell him over the computer. Even though that's how we'd been communicating half the time, it seemed so impersonal.

I'm not disappointed. Just overwhelmed. We'll talk tomorrow, yes?

So you're coming tomorrow night?

To the vague event with the address?

Yes.

I'll be there.

TWENTY-SIX

I dreaded getting in the car the next morning with Amelia. I had no idea what to say. A conversation with her could wait until after I'd had one with DJ. There was nothing wrong with that. When I got into her car, I immediately felt bad.

And of course, the first thing she asked was, "So did Heath Hall slip up at all last night?" She eased out of my driveway.

"No. I'm still not sure who he is." That was sort of true. I was maybe 10 percent not sure.

She smiled. "Well, I spent an hour talking to Robert yesterday after school."

"After school you drove me home."

"I came back and met him after track practice."

"Oh yeah? What did he say?"

"He was like a vault, but I think he knows something. He got this sly smile when I mentioned that truth quote you said about the sun and the moon."

"He did? So you think it's him?" As much as I hadn't wanted it to be him the day before, now anyone other than DJ would be welcome news.

"I think it could be him. Did you talk to Jackson?"

"No, I didn't get a chance."

We pulled in to the parking lot and I claimed I had to talk to a teacher before the bell rang. But DJ wasn't in the coach's office. Why did he pick today of all days to really not-work? Didn't he want to talk to me before tonight? Before I had to see him again with that mask on. Was I supposed to pretend I didn't know him?

A growl escaped my throat and I headed for my first-period class.

"Moore!" The call must've been loud because I heard it through my music. I clicked the off button and turned.

Jackson was heading my way at a slow jog. My heart gave a little leap.

"Hey, Holt."

He had his mischief-making smile on. "You're not the only one who can figure things out."

I stopped in the middle of the hall. "What?"

He held up the Styrofoam cup I hadn't seen until then. "Norman's. I don't believe you went to that seedy shop for me."

"Oh. Right. You found it." If that had been Jackson last night online, he'd mention it now, wouldn't he? I stared at him, willing him to say something. He just had his easy smile on.

"You no longer own me." He took a sip, then met my eyes. "Unless you want to."

My heart thudded twice. I wasn't sure if he was just being his jokester self right now or if he was being serious. "I . . ."

The bell rang. "We'll talk later, Moore," he said, then held up his cup again. "To heaven in a cup." Then he turned and jogged away. No, that boy did not need to put on a mask to speak his mind. There was no way he was Heath Hall.

Only we didn't talk later. And DJ never showed up at school, so I couldn't talk to him. Now I was facing the night, the Heath Hall event, blind. My shoulders were acting up. I needed some aspirin. Amelia dropped her bag in the middle of my bedroom floor. "Due to the vagueness of tonight's event, I had no idea what to wear. What are you wearing?"

"Jeans and a nice shirt. I think."

"Good call. An in-between outfit." She opened her bag and began flinging clothes onto my bed. "I don't believe your parents left you alone for the weekend."

"One night."

"My parents would never trust me enough to leave me home alone. They would think I'd throw a party or something." She stopped and put her hands on her hips. "We should throw a party. We can invite everyone over after the Heath Hall thing tonight."

"Probably not a good idea."

"You're right. We'll just invite a few people over."

I laughed and sifted through the clothes in my closet until I found the green blouse I was looking for. "Nobody over. But that doesn't mean we can't stay out late."

"So true."

I needed to tell Amelia now before we left. Before we saw Heath Hall. Why was I still calling him that? DJ. Before we saw DJ, I needed to prepare her for who he was. Tell her how I pieced together the clues: how long ago the account was created and how he talked to his dog and I soaked his sweater and how he and the masked man were never in the same room at the same time. And

I needed to tell her . . . how he felt about me.

"Do you think tonight is the night that Heath Hall will unmask himself? Maybe that's why the description was so vague."

"No. I don't." As I said it, I realized I believed that. If he hadn't done it in five years, why would he do it now? I could still wait to talk to Amelia until after I'd talked to DJ. I hoped that once we talked, things could still work out with him and Amelia. If he knew how I felt and how she felt, it would clear things up. Everything would turn out fine. Yes, that's what I'd do.

We sat in a small theater in the old town district. The only people there were Heath Hall supporters, and it was a fairly small crowd at that. Twenty? All faces I recognized. Dylan, Brady, even Robert, who I could now officially eliminate as a suspect. Amelia was surprised to see him there after her talk with him the day before. Maybe the numbers were few because this event seemed even more vague than the others.

The heavy velvet green curtain was open and a single spotlight lit a mic on the stage. Whatever DJ was doing involved that mic. Singing? Speaking?

There were empty chairs on either side of us and Amelia kept looking back toward the door like she thought he'd walk in that way. I figured he'd walk in from backstage, so I didn't bother craning my neck around.

"You think he'll make us sit here for three hours?"

"I hope not."

"Maybe he's waiting for more people to show up."

"Yeah, maybe." But right as I said it, footsteps sounded on the hardwood of the stage and Heath Hall appeared from behind the side curtain. He walked to the mic, tapped it twice, then cleared his throat.

"Tonight I have a declaration. A truth I need to speak that I haven't been able to as myself."

This was different. But he'd said the mask wasn't just about expressing fears. That was just one of its purposes. So tonight we got a truth.

"A poem," he continued. "Declaring truth. Revealing love. In front of all. It's from my heart. From my soul."

It took my brain a moment to realize he had already started the poem. He was midpoem. And he was about to say something he couldn't say in front of anybody but especially not Amelia. He was going to say he liked me. I stood up and screamed, "No!"

He stopped. The microphone issued a screech of feedback.

Amelia tugged on my arm and whispered, "What are you doing?"

The rest of the room had turned to look at me as well. I was supposed to say something now. Justify why I'd stopped Heath Hall from speaking. I didn't want to have to tell him that I didn't feel the same way. I wanted to pull him off the stage and talk privately to him, spare the embarrassment. If he needed a mask to say it, he was already feeling unsure. I wished I didn't have to do this, but Amelia and her feelings were the most important thing to me right now.

Out of the corner of my eye I saw a movement, someone sitting down next to Amelia. Then I heard that someone whisper, "Sorry I'm late. What did I miss?"

I turned toward that someone, who was now slipping his hand into Amelia's.

"DJ?"

He smiled up at me. "Hi, Hadley."

"Oh no." My eyes whipped back to the stage. Heath Hall still stared at me and appeared to have lost every ounce of the confidence he had when he first got on the stage. I held up my hands. "I'm so sorry. I thought you were someone else." Why did I say that out loud to the only person possibly left who could be under that mask? The person I had wanted to be under that mask all along. Was it too late for him to finish what he'd started? "Go on. I'm listening. It was really good." But he was still frozen, now gripping the mic stand. I gave him my pleading eyes. "Please. Finish."

From behind me someone called out, "You can do

it. Keep going." I recognized that voice. It felt like the world stopped spinning or some other phenomenon that would explain why I was suddenly dizzy and lost my balance. I braced myself on the back of the seat in front of me. I turned toward the voice behind me.

Jackson.

He winked at me. Then it seemed to register to him that I was standing up. That I was the person who had called out to stop Heath Hall from speaking. He gave me a questioning head tilt. My gaze shot from him to DJ to Robert (still sitting a few rows up from us) and finally to the still-silent Heath Hall. Who was he?

"He's not any of them," I whispered to Amelia.

"Huh." She didn't seem as concerned about this development as I was. "Back to the drawing board, I guess."

I sidestepped out of the row, Amelia stage-whispering to me the whole time to stay.

That guy on stage thought I knew him? That's what he'd said in our chats. Was he about to profess his love to me up there? I couldn't let that happen. Once I was clear of the seats, I ran out the back door and to Amelia's car, where I leaned against the bumper and waited for things to make sense or for me to be magically transported out of the parking lot to save me from the humiliation that I was sure was about to occur.

TWENTY-SEVEN

I thought Amelia would come out first to find me, or the masked man, but it was Jackson.

"Hey, Moore. Everything okay?" He slid his arm around my shoulders and I leaned into him.

I had never asked him. I'd asked a lot of people if they knew who Heath Hall was, but it occurred to me that I'd never asked him. Why hadn't I just asked him to save myself from this humiliation? He would've told me. He liked me. "You know. Who was that in there on the stage? Who is Heath Hall?"

"You know I can't tell you that."

I pushed away from him, hurt. "You too?" I stood and paced. "Is this all just some big joke to you? Let's make Hadley look like a fool for fun because my life is only about discovering the ultimate prank? I just want to go home. Why don't I have a car so I can go home?"

"Because your brother owns your car, and you're too afraid to confront your parents about it."

I narrowed my eyes at him. "Don't throw my secrets at me when you won't tell me yours."

He pressed his palms to his temples, then pointed back at the theater. "I can't tell you his secret. That's not mine to tell. Why do you care who he is anyway?"

"Because . . ." I wanted to know who I'd been talking to for the last month, who I'd told things to, who apparently liked me.

"Great reason," he mumbled.

"I owe you nothing."

His expression flattened in obvious hurt.

"I'm going home." I marched back to the theater and found Amelia. The stage was now empty, but people were visiting around the room. Amelia and DJ were still linked by their hands. When had that happened anyway? She'd actually done it, was dating her unattainable crush.

"You should've seen that," Amelia said when I was at her side. "He just told everyone he was gay. He said that saying it out loud with the mask on would give him the courage to do it without the mask soon."

I stared at the empty stage, confused. Heath Hall didn't like me? So what did he mean the day before in our chat when he said everyone noticed me? Amelia was staring at me now, concerned. "That's cool," I managed to say. And it was cool. I was proud of him.

"It was so inspiring." Her brain was making some jumps too. "I guess that's another clue for us."

"Can you take me home?"

"What? Are you okay? You don't look so good."

"I just want to go home."

Amelia tugged on DJ's arm. "Sorry. We'll have to meet up another night."

"You can go out with DJ. I don't need you with me. Can you just drop me off?"

"Are you sure?"

"Yes, I'm going to sleep."

The whole way home Amelia kept asking me over and over if I wanted her to stay with me. Over and over I assured her that I didn't.

As we turned onto my street, I asked, "When? You and DJ?" Apparently, I couldn't speak in complete sentences anymore.

"In the course of me trying to find out if he was Heath Hall yesterday and today."

"DJ wasn't on your list!" I said, shocked.

"He wasn't at first, but then I remembered he was at the pool the first time you saw Heath Hall and he was at the museum that night but we had left him. Then at the bungee jump he had completely disappeared."

"So you thought it might be him?"

"I did at first, but not after we talked a couple times."

"Oh. Good."

"Are you good? Because I can stay." She stopped in front of my house.

"You will drive me nuts if you stay. You know where the spare key is. Let yourself in later. I'll be asleep."

"You're the best friend ever."

"I know."

My plan when I went inside was not to look online. To do just what I said I was going to do and crawl in bed. But it was like a sickness. I couldn't help myself. After brushing my teeth and changing my button-down blouse for a comfortable T-shirt, I pulled up the one waiting message on my phone. It was from Heath Hall.

You want a car, Moore? Go get your car.

What? Had Jackson taken over Heath Hall's account? I read the two sentences again. Go get my car? I stood slowly, slipped on a pair of flip-flops, and went outside. Nobody was there. I started to walk back inside when what Jackson had said out in the parking lot came back to me. *Your brother owns your car.*

My brother's truck sat like it always did on its raised platform. On the hood I could barely make out a dark object. I slowly approached. It was a black backpack, a long white envelope jutting out of the pocket. On the front of that envelope my first and last name were written in Sharpie. I opened it up and unfolded the single sheet of paper inside.

You were nominated to be Heath Hall by a
previous embodiment. The request stated that
you were too set on a singular goal. You needed
to expand your focus. That need was evaluated
and found false. But upon further observation, a
different need was discovered. You need to stop
trying to make up for the past. Stop competing
with the past in a game you can't win. You need
to live in the present and own your place there
in the lives of those around you. You need to let
go of your fear of acceptance, let people in, and
demand what's yours. You can choose to accept
this challenge by completing an act you feel
best symbolizes overcoming your fear. You can
do it alone or have the group to support you by
emailing your act to I__am__HeathHall@gmail.com.
When the mask has served its purpose or if you

choose not to accept this challenge, please return, by way of enclosed lockbox key to the address inside.

I opened the backpack to find the Heath Hall mask.

A need. I now had a need and got to know the secret.

No wonder everyone thought Heath Hall was someone different. He was. He was many different people. One jumped into the pool, another showed his art, another bungee jumped. And tonight, Jackson couldn't tell me who was on that stage. It wasn't his secret to tell. But that didn't matter right now. What mattered was who was behind the private messages. That was Jackson. I looked at the note again. Was this him too? Did the goof-off Jackson organize this device to help people work through their fears? Like Dumbo's black feather, he had said to me once. I laughed, but then I stopped as I took in my brother's truck.

I knew what Jackson wanted me to do. He wanted me to drive it. To go get the keys from inside that little glass box and drive this truck off its platform. It would definitely be symbolic. Me facing my brother. Now I knew why that guy's hands were shaking in the back corridor of the museum. These weren't average fears being targeted. This was the worst fear I could possibly imagine. In so many ways. No wonder the people who had been

Heath Hall before kept this secret. They understood how serious this was.

I zipped up the backpack, the Heath Hall mask still inside, and went back in the house. I just wanted to go to my room and pretend this hadn't happened. It killed me to disappoint Jackson.

This was unfair. Other people wouldn't care what Jackson thought of them if they did or didn't do it. Did other people even know Jackson was involved? I was almost positive they didn't. I set the backpack on the kitchen counter and stared at my brother's keys on the wall. The truck probably wouldn't even start. It had been a month since my dad had charged the battery. All I had to do was climb in, turn the key, and when it didn't start, climb out. That was facing a fear.

Before I could talk myself out of it, I opened the glass box and grabbed the keys off the hook. This was the first time I'd ever held them. When they didn't burn a hole through my palm, I carried them outside along with the backpack and my purse and I stared at the truck some more. That platform was high. Several feet off the ground. And it didn't have a ramp or anything. If I got the truck started, would I be able to drive it off without damaging it? And how would I get it back up before my parents got home?

It wasn't going to start, so none of this mattered. I took

a deep breath, opened the driver's-side door, and climbed inside. That wasn't too hard. I unzipped the backpack and pulled out the mask of Heath Hall. "There's no way I'm wearing you, dude, but you can have a front row seat for the action." I propped the mask up on the dash. It was about the spirit of the challenge, not actually having to wear the mask, right?

"Okay, Moore," I said to myself, "just put the key in and turn." My hands were shaking more than those of the museum Heath Hall that night. I couldn't even still mine enough to insert the key in the ignition. I took several deep breaths. Finally, the key slid in. I pressed on the brake and turned the key. The engine sputtered but then caught. My heart doubled in speed. No. It wasn't supposed to start. I hit the wheel. I really hated this truck.

There was no way I could drive it. "Why?" I asked, playing the other side of an argument against myself that I didn't want to have. "Because they'll know," I answered.

Wasn't that the point? The point of facing my fear, of coming out of the past? But no, it wasn't about my parents. It was about me facing my brother. I could drive the truck and put it back. My dad had to have some ramps in the garage. How else would he have gotten it up here in the first place? Yes, that's what I'd do.

I turned off the ignition and my heart immediately calmed. A check of the garage found exactly what I was looking for. Two rusty ramps. I dragged them out of their corner and across the lawn, wiping spiderwebs and dust off my jeans as I did. When I made it back to the truck, I plopped them down with a deep breath. Now I wouldn't damage the truck by driving it off.

I lined up one ramp in front of each of the front wheels and then returned to the cab of the truck. Maybe it wouldn't start now. No such luck. The hum of the engine vibrated through my legs and back. I almost turned it off again. I couldn't do this. Heath Hall stared at me from the dash, daring me to, reminding me of how many fears he'd successfully faced in the past. "I don't need you judging me, Heath." I was stalling. I was chickening out. "Okay, stupid feather, give me some power." I grabbed the mask and pulled it on.

TWENTY-EIGHT

It was hot in the mask, my breath making it stuffy. Plus, the eyeholes weren't very big. It was hard to see out. I tugged at the neck to readjust it on my face, which helped a little with my vision. My parents were going to kill me if they found out. They were going to see that I was irresponsible and selfish. They were going to wish him back all over again.

"No. I will not compete with you anymore, Eric."

Besides, I wasn't doing this. Heath Hall was. I laughed at my own thoughts, knowing my fear had officially taken over.

Don't analyze, just drive, I told myself. I pushed on the gas and the truck lurched forward. The ramps were a little lower than the platform and the truck dropped a few inches before easing down. My stomach dropped even further. But then I was off the platform and on the street and my nerves seemed to settle. I was still hot and couldn't breathe, so I ripped the mask off and propped it back on the dash. "You did your job, Heath Hall. Thank you."

I was two blocks away from my house before I began to wonder how long this drive had to last. The shock of the entire night had started to wear off, and I was left with the memory of how I had been so mean to Jackson. I'd told him I owed him nothing. He had just been trying to protect someone's privacy. An apology was in order.

I found myself driving to Norman's because a good apology is always accompanied by a bribe. It wasn't until I was waiting for my drink that I realized I had no idea where Jackson lived.

I pulled out my phone. I didn't have his number. How had we never exchanged numbers? Oh, that's right. I spent weeks being annoyed by him.

Hadn't Amelia claimed that the internet knew all? What did I have to lose? I typed in a quick message. *Hey, does anyone know where Jackson Holt lives? Private message me his address.*

By the time I'd ordered the cider, I'd already gotten three DMs. It didn't even disturb me that they were all from girls. Okay, it kind of did.

I collected his drink and left.

Even though the radio in my brother's truck looked newer than the truck itself, it was still older than dirt. When I powered it on, it only let out a static buzzing. Several black buttons jutted out from the bottom. I pressed each one and the red line in front of the numbers moved, but still the radio emitted nothing but static. It had a tape deck as well. I wondered if that worked. Not that I had tapes. And of course there was no way to plug in my phone. If ever there was a time I'd needed music to block out my thoughts, it was now. I didn't just have to worry about how tonight might end but also how driving to Jackson's house, uninvited, might too. I went anyway. It was a night of facing fears, after all.

It wasn't very cold out, but I stood on his porch, clutching his drink, shivering. My teeth clattered together and everything. I felt like I did after a tough swim day, standing outside the pool, still dripping wet. I hated being vulnerable, putting myself out there. I hated looking stupid, feeling stupid. I didn't want to do this. But I had to. I would.

I took a deep breath, put my game face on, and knocked.

A woman opened the door and gave me a tentative smile.

"Is Jackson here?" I asked.

She flipped her wrist to check her watch. It was only a little after nine on a Friday night. Was she going to turn me away? "I think he might be asleep," she said.

Disappointment settled onto my chest. I wasn't sure if my face changed with the feeling or not, but she said, "Let me go check." She closed the door halfway, then left.

A couple minutes later the door squeaked open again and Jackson stood there in some too-small sweats and a T-shirt. I gave him my confident look: shoulders back, sure smile on my face. He ran his hand through his hair, making it stand up, and a guarded smile came onto his face. "Moore. You're here." He glanced over my shoulder and saw the truck parked against the curb in front of his house and his smile widened. "You did it."

"Barely." I thrust the drink forward. "This is for you. An I-was-a-jerk-again bribe. I'm sorry for what I said in the parking lot."

He shrugged. "You've labeled me as a slacker, and you're sticking by it. I appreciate the consistency."

He wasn't going to accept my apology or the drink I was still holding out. "At least take this. You know I can't drink it. It's disgusting."

He laughed and took the drink.

"Thank you." I turned and walked away.

"Moore?"

I stopped but didn't turn.

"Where are you going?"

"I'm not sure."

"Do you want me to come?"

I put my head down, letting that confident front drop for a moment as utter relief poured through my body. At least he couldn't see my face.

"Is that a no?" he asked.

"Yes—no—I mean, please. I want you to come."

"Let me grab some shoes. I'll meet you out there."

Just seconds after I climbed into the cab, he did too, holding a pair of Converse in one hand and his drink in the other. He almost sat on the box my mom had placed inside weeks ago but slid it over to the middle just in time.

"You know I only agreed so I could sit in this truck, right?"

Right. I had forgotten about his love of this truck.

"A joke. After all this time and you constantly reminding me that I joke about everything, you don't get my joke?"

I choked out a weird sputtering laugh.

"Are you freaking out?" He studied me closer, then cussed. "You're freaking out."

"No. I'm fine."

He let out a single laugh. "Fine, huh? Okay, take a deep breath." He dropped his shoes on the floor and his hand went to my neck, where he began to massage. "Just breathe." He turned on the radio but the static was still the only noise it would produce. I loved that he knew music would've helped. But there was no music. Only deafening silence filled with the thoughts of how stupid this was.

"My parents are going to kill me," I said.

"Your parents are not going to kill you."

"My mom will for sure. My dad will just be very disappointed. He is really, really good at being disappointed."

"You're in your head too much. Don't think about that. Think about the good that will come of this."

"There is no good. Only death."

I could tell he was trying not to, but he laughed. "Do you want to take it back? I can help you take it back."

Yes. I wanted to take the truck back and pretend none of this ever happened. My eyes landed on the mask still sitting on the dashboard. Maybe it really did possess some secret power, because I took a deep breath and shook my head no. "I'm here. Let's have some fun." Besides, I'd already decided this wasn't about my parents. This was about me facing my brother. Facing what I'd competed with my whole life. When the night was over, I was going to put the truck back as if it was never moved. The thought gave me new determination. Tonight would give me the strength to face my parents. To let them know how I felt.

"Heath Hall is sitting on your dashboard," Jackson said. "That's kind of creepy."

"Hey, you're the one who started the whole thing."

"Actually, I wasn't."

"Okay, you talk, I'll drive." I turned the key, the truck rumbling to life, and we pulled away from his house.

His hand dropped from my neck and he reached down to pull on his shoes. "I've been the Heath Hall caretaker for about six months now. I think someone, much like you, thought I was a bit irresponsible and wanted me to step outside myself."

"What do you mean, someone? You don't know who?"

"I don't know who."

"So wait. You never needed to use the mask; you just got put in charge of it?"

"I think I needed it more than anyone. My fear, my truth, was bigger than one event. I had to see myself through the fears others faced."

"What was your fear?"

"You nailed me on the head, Moore. That's why it was so hard to hear. I thought I'd grown these last six months, but I haven't. I have no ambitions. I don't know who I am or what I want to do with my life."

"A lot of people don't know that. There's nothing wrong with that."

"Where I differ from others is that I don't care."

I stared out at the dark road in front of me. "I don't believe you."

"Oh, but you do, because every time you're mad at me, the truth comes out."

I felt bad for throwing that in his face a couple times now when it was obviously something he struggled with. "No. I mean, sometimes you like to goof off, and when my awful temper comes out because I'm hurt or whatever, I say that, but I don't think that's you."

"What's me, then?"

"You care about people. Look at what you're doing for me tonight."

"That's because I like you, Moore. It's completely selfish."

"So did you like Painter Boy and Suck It Guy too?"

"Suck It Guy?"

"You know, 'Suck it, fear!'" I rolled my eyes.

He laughed. "Oh, you mean Suck It Girl."

"That was a girl?"

"Yep. People's brains perceive things how they want to perceive things. You'd assigned Heath Hall a gender, so you didn't analyze the evidence right."

"Huh. Weird."

"Wait . . . you thought it was me that night, didn't you? Did you think I was *all* the versions of Heath Hall?"

"Yes."

"I thought you totally figured out that it was more than one person because of the things you said over private message. That's why I told you."

"What things did I say? The dog thing?"

"No. You said, 'like Dumbo's black feather,' and that the mask helped others reveal their fears too. I thought you figured it out."

"I meant the mask, you, the private-message thing was helping me reveal my fears . . . to you."

"Oh. Yeah, no. I didn't get that."

I laughed. "By the way, that mask is hot. And not looks-wise."

"You wore it?"

"It helped me drive the truck off the platform."

He smiled and stared at the mask for a long moment. "There's just something about it, right? The spirit of the spy hero Heath Hall must live in there somewhere. And knowing the mask has been there while so many people

faced what's scared them. Revealed something important. It's almost like it really does have some power."

For once, I didn't think Jackson was kidding, and I
agreed with him.

TWENTY-NINE

"So where are we going, Moore?"

"What time do you have to be back?" I asked.

"My curfew is midnight."

"Then I want to go everywhere I've ever wanted to go."

He laughed. "Not sure if we can accomplish that very general goal in three hours."

"No, it's actually quite specific. Every time I've wanted to go somewhere but have been stuck because I didn't have a car. That's where we are going tonight."

"So Disneyland from when you were five?"

"No, I just mean since I've had a license. So the last ten months."

"Got it. Sounds awesome."

"First stop." I pulled into the 7-Eleven parking lot.

"Seven-Eleven?"

"Have you ever gotten a craving so bad that you still remember it ten months later?"

He raised his eyebrows at me in the teasing way he had. "Yes, I have."

I hit his arm. I really couldn't tell if he treated me differently than he did everyone else or not. "Stop teasing me. I'm on a mission."

"Wait, we can't tease on this mission?"

I didn't answer, just got out of the truck. When he caught up with me, I said, "There's a corner gas station right up the street from our house that I can walk to, but they do not carry everything."

"Am I about to find out your favorite drink so I can own you?"

"You could only own me if I didn't know where it was sold."

"Not true. We just established that this drink is only gettable by car. You, my friend, don't have one of those."

"It doesn't matter, I've given it up." I cut through the candy aisle and headed to the back.

"You've given up your favorite drink?"

"I've given up sugar."

"So why are we here?"

I reached the Slurpee machine, grabbed a cup, and went straight for the lime. "Because tonight we're breaking all the rules." I smiled at him as I filled the cup. "You see, Jackson, the smart people who live somewhere warm have a favorite drink that is cold."

"That does sound more practical." He snatched the now-full cup from me. "Well, it's my turn to buy since you're a drink ahead of me."

"No, mine were payback."

He just headed for the register. After paying and on our way back to the truck, I remembered something from the letter I got with the mask. "So just anyone can nominate anyone to wear the mask?"

"No, it has to be someone who has worn the mask before."

We climbed into the truck and buckled our seat belts.

"Huh. So who nominated me?" I took a long sip of my drink.

"Technically, I'm not supposed to tell you."

I stuck the key in the ignition. "But . . . ?"

"But I will."

I waited, and when he didn't say anything, I turned toward him with raised eyebrows.

"It was Pool Boy."

"What?" I asked, confused.

"I really didn't know you very well at the time or Pool Boy, so I thought his claimed fear of body image issues was real, but later, after I got your DM about how I should stay away from the pool . . ." He smiled at that memory. "After I learned Pool Boy's relationship to you, I realized the fear was probably a lie."

"His relationship to me . . . ?"

Jackson waited for me to come to the realization, and when I finally did, I gasped. "Pool Boy is *Robert*? Robert ruined my race. What a . . ."

"Jerk? Yeah. I normally wouldn't tell the nominee about the nominator, but since I'm pretty sure that whole stunt had nothing to do with his fear and he only did it to mess with you, I just wanted to make sure you knew . . . in case . . . I don't know . . . you were thinking about getting back together with him or something." He held my gaze.

"You think I was thinking about getting back together with him?"

"I saw you two in the hall the other day and . . ." He shrugged. "You looked kind of cozy."

He was noticing me in the hall with other guys? "We're not getting back together." I should've been even more mad right now at Robert for ruining my race that night over a month ago, but I found that I really was over it, over him. Wasting energy on him seemed pointless.

"I knew you were smarter than that."

"Sometimes I am. Obviously not in the figuring-out-the-Heath-Hall-mystery department."

"Nobody figures it out until the mask ends up in their possession."

I took another long drink, my throat going cold, my jaw aching with the sugar. It tasted amazing.

Jackson laughed. "That good, huh?"

"What? Did I make a noise?"

"The kind that said sugar was back in your life to stay."

"Funny." I propped the drink between my knees and started the truck. "How did the whole Heath Hall thing start anyway? Do you know? The social media account was established five years ago. That's why I thought it was someone older, like DJ."

"Did you want Heath Hall to be the dreamy DJ?"

"No. I didn't." *I wanted him to be you.* That's what I should've said, but I still didn't quite know where we stood. We were firmly in friend territory and I couldn't tell if he wanted to be more than that. I pulled out of the parking lot.

"How did it start? Well, legend is that someone dressed up as Heath for Halloween one year. Obviously someone with some money to throw around because they got the best-quality mask ever. If you remember, that was the year the first Heath Hall movie came out and it opened big."

"Take Down."

"That's the title of the movie, right? I've never actually seen it."

I laughed. "You, the caretaker of Heath Hall this year, have never seen how he came to be?"

"I know. It's a tragedy. But anyway, I guess there was this car full of people driving around that Halloween night and there was an attempted carjacking. Some guy with a gun came up to the window and tried to force everyone out of the car. So Heath Hall, well, the person dressed up as him, was driving in a car behind theirs and got out and tackled the guy, disarmed him, then left before anyone knew who he was. It kind of became this legend after that. I don't know if someone else got a different mask and started passing it around or if the original guy thought he would give other people a chance to face a fear while wearing the mask or maybe that whole story was just made up by the person who thought of the idea, but whatever the case, that's the history."

"How come I've never heard that story?"

"Because it happened in a completely different city over five years ago. Heath Hall has traveled from there to here."

"How do you know all that, then?"

"The story gets passed on to the keeper of the mask. I guess it's supposed to make us want to be noble or keep the secret or I'm not really sure, but it works."

"I can see that. It's a pretty cool story. And I can see how the wearers of the mask would want to keep the secret too. There's this kind of reverence that comes after having to use it. A respect. Like a secret society."

"Some people talk. You were asking around; you probably know that."

I was about to tell him that nobody had told us anything but then remembered he was right: people had named names. But because there had been so many different names named, we hadn't thought any of them were right. Now I realized they all had been right. There were many different Heath Halls.

I pulled into the parking lot.

Jackson gazed out the window, then turned to me, disappointed. "Are we at school?"

"Sort of. Well, obviously we're at school, but not because I've ever had a deep desire to come to school when I've been car-less, but because this is where my second home lives." I drove through the lot and parked close to the walk that led to the pool.

"Oh. Of course."

I unbuckled my seat belt.

"Are we getting out? It looks locked," he asked.

"I have a key."

He joined me outside and we headed toward the gate. "How do you have a key?"

"I swim a lot. I needed one."

"Did you *steal* a key, Moore?"

I handed him my Slurpee so I could unlock the gate. "Stealing is such a strong word."

He took a sip of my drink, then stuck his tongue out. "That is sour."

"I think you mean delicious." I took it back.

The pool was dark, but the smell of chlorine was so familiar that my body relaxed another degree. I wished I had brought my suit.

"I don't believe you stole a key. I never would've suspected that of you. You're so . . ."

"So what?"

"Nothing."

"Finish your thought. I deserve whatever adjective was coming next after all the things I've called you."

"It's not a bad thing. It's just you're so good . . . perfect."

"Hey, I just stole a truck."

He laughed. "I know! You even excel in the fear-facing department."

"I needed a mask to face my fears. I'm obviously not perfect."

"The only reason you need the mask is because you're afraid of not being perfect."

"Not true." I said it but only halfheartedly. That was mostly right. "But either way, I'm not."

"You're Moore."

I rolled up my jeans and sat on the edge of the pool. "What does that mean?"

"Amelia was wrong about why I call you Moore. If I tell you why I really call you that, you promise not to hate me?"

"I promise. Unless it's really bad. Then I'll hate you."

He pulled up his sweats and sat down next to me. "Okay, it started off as a joke."

"Not surprising." It used to sound mocking every time he'd said it.

"Because your last name fit your personality so well. You always have to do more and be better at everything than everyone else."

I gasped. "Rude."

"Motivation isn't a bad thing. I think I was jealous of it. Then I got to know you, and realized you *are* more. So it fit."

I kicked my foot and splashed him with water. He held up his hands to block the spray. Then he jumped up to a squat, wrapped his arm around my waist, and dragged me back so I couldn't do it again. In the process, he lost his footing and stumbled back, me falling against him so we were both sitting again, me now nestled between his knees. I struggled to get free, but he held me tight from behind. He rested his chin on my shoulder. "No more water, fish."

I relaxed, letting him hold me, my back running the length of his chest. He felt solid and soft at the same time. "How did you know that driving the truck would be the hardest thing for me to do?"

A light cut through the black of the pool. "Who's out there?" a deep voice called out past the fence.

I laughed and Jackson stood, pulling me up with him.

"It's just Marvin," I said. "The janitor. He likes me."

"Does everyone like you?"

"I could ask you the same question."

"I don't know that it would have the same answer."

I turned to face him. Did he really not think people liked him? Everyone liked him. I was the one that everyone thought was a closed-off jerk.

"Hello?" Marvin called again.

"Just me!" I yelled to Marvin, still looking at Jackson. "Hadley Moore."

Jackson smiled his sly smile at me. "So much more," he whispered.

THIRTY

Back in the truck, Jackson was messing with the radio again when suddenly music blasted through the cab so loud that I almost swerved off the road.

"Sorry, sorry," he said, quickly adjusting the volume.

"How did you get it to work?" I asked.

"I don't know. This button here."

"Cool." I drummed my fingers on the steering wheel to an old classic rock song.

"What's this?" Jackson tapped the top of the cardboard box on the seat between us.

"My brother."

"Whoa." He held up his hands. "Your brother's ashes are in this truck?"

"No. It's this thing we do every year for him. A mini memorial service. My mom and sometimes my dad pick out a few things that remind them of Eric. Then we wake up on his death day and talk about him and put the box in the truck. Then we go eat his favorite food."

"Wow, that's more than my parents do on my birthday."

"It's pretty elaborate."

He pulled the box onto his lap, then paused with his hands on either side of the lid. "May I?"

"Sure. It's nothing earth-shattering."

He opened it and looked inside. First he pulled out the picture of my brother and his prom date. "Check out that hair."

I laughed.

"So this is him?"

"That's him."

"The golden child."

"Yep. You should hear the stories. He did no wrong."

"You grew up on those stories?"

"Yes."

"No wonder you feel the need to be perfect. You

thought he was. You have to live up to that."

I didn't say anything. The truck rumbled in the silence, headlights cutting through the blackness beyond the windshield.

"You know he wasn't perfect, right? You know he had faults and made mistakes and probably made your parents mad a lot, but they don't remember all that anymore."

"I don't know that. I never knew him."

"I didn't either and I know it's true. Even if they did remember those things, they wouldn't talk about them now. He's dead."

"I know."

"I'm being insensitive. I just find myself getting defensive on your behalf. I'm sorry."

"Most of the time, when I think about my brother, I feel nothing. Sometimes I feel jealousy and sometimes I wish him out of existence, which makes no sense because he doesn't exist."

"It makes sense."

"Thank you."

He put the picture down and picked up the movie. "How does this represent your brother?"

"I guess he liked spy movies. He probably would've loved Heath Hall." I patted the mask on the dashboard.

"*The Hunt for Red October.* Is it any good?"

"Never seen it."

The last thing he brought out was the squirt gun, which he immediately shot at me. A spray of water hit my hair. "It's loaded. Your mom actually loaded it."

"I see that." I wiped the side of my face where it had dripped.

He shot me again.

I reached over and hit him.

He laughed. "I thought you liked water."

"Ha-ha."

"Does this have to do with the spy movies?"

"No."

"He liked water? Like you?"

"Nope."

He dropped the gun back in the box. "You going to keep me in suspense?"

"Remember when you met my dad?"

"Of course."

"When you left, the first thing my dad said to me was, 'I've never met someone who reminded me more of your brother.'"

He squeezed his eyes shut. "And then you hated me even more."

"No. You already bugged me. I guess that was when I realized I would've hated my brother had I known him.

And that made me mad at you, yes."

"So see, your brother wasn't perfect. He was an irresponsible goofball with no idea about his future." He nodded toward the squirt gun, the representation of that playful nature.

"He knew he wasn't going to have a future."

Again Jackson squeezed his eyes shut and put the lid back on the box. "Sorry."

"No, don't be. Here's the thing. My whole life, I've never felt close to my brother. Never felt like I knew him at all. I knew facts about him but couldn't picture him. Then you came along in all your annoyingness and my dad put a personality to him. I hated that at first. And if I'm being honest, I kind of reveled in it too because I realized that I wanted to hate him. But now. Now that I know you better, I know that my brother and I would've been great friends." For the first time, maybe ever, I felt my eyes prick with tears over the thought of missing out on that friendship with him. "So I know this is weird, but thank you for that."

He slowly set the box back on the seat between us. "Great. I just got put in the 'he's like a brother to me' category."

I laughed. "You're good for me."

"How so?"

"Because you can make me laugh." Especially when I

had just been on the verge of tears.

"Oh, did you think that was a joke?"

I laughed again. "See?"

Nirvana came on the radio and Jackson turned up the volume.

THIRTY-ONE

Considering it was only ten thirty, the neighborhood was quiet. The porch light was the only thing that lit the house. All the other windows were dark.

"Where are we?" he asked.

"Amelia's house."

"Are we picking up Amelia?"

"Nope. She's spending the night at my house. And considering she hasn't texted me to find out where I am, she must still be out with DJ."

"So we're going to hang out with Amelia's parents?"

"Amelia lives four miles from me. A little too far to

walk. Without a car, I can't see my best friend whenever I want to. I have to depend on her driving everywhere. In junior high sometimes I'd ride my bike here but even that took a while."

"How long have you known Amelia?"

"Since the second grade. She has the most awesome tree house. We'd spend hours back there."

"Are you going to show it to me?"

"I wasn't planning on it."

"You just throw out the words 'awesome tree house' and we are going to walk away?"

"Fine. Come on." As we walked toward her side gate, I said, "It's been a long time since I've been in it. It could've been my younger brain that found it awesome and now it will be lame."

"Backpedaling already?"

We got to the gate and I gestured for him to reach over to undo the latch as I shined my phone for him to see. Soon we were in her backyard. It really had been a while since I'd been back there. But my memory wasn't wrong. The tree house *was* awesome. It was built around a giant oak tree in the center of her yard. The back patio light was just bright enough for us to make it out.

"Wow," he breathed. "You almost didn't let me see this. There's a way to get up there, right?"

"There used to be a ladder attached on the back." I was

already walking as I said this, and when I rounded the tree, I saw the ladder still there, waiting to be climbed. I went first, ascending the thirty steps. No wonder Amelia's mom was always nervous when we were out here: this thing was high. Jackson followed close behind. It was more of a deck than a house. It had no roof, but a railing surrounded the wooden platform. It was dusty and some boards were rotted through, but when Jackson reached the top, he immediately lay on his back, putting his hands behind his head.

"If this were in my backyard, I'd be up here every day."

And I believed he would. His joy was contagious. I took a spot next to him and stared into the dark twisted branches above us. Last time I'd tried to relax and enjoy a moment of beauty like this, my body wouldn't let me. This time, I felt like I wanted to stay here forever.

"Do you hear that?" he asked.

I didn't hear anything at first, but when I listened closely, I could barely make out music coming from another backyard. "Someone is having a party."

"The song is in Spanish."

I listened closer and sure enough, the words were in a different language. "Do you know any Spanish?" I asked.

"I've taken two years in school. So no."

I smiled. "I was dumb and took French. We live in

California. Who doesn't take Spanish when you live in California?" I wasn't sure if I was listening harder or someone turned up the music, but it got a little louder.

"When did you realize you were good at swimming? That it was something you could excel in?"

"Summer before sixth grade I beat a seventh grader in the one-hundred-meter butterfly. It's a hard stroke for a kid so young and I beat her. That day I made it my goal to be good enough to swim once I got to college."

"In the sixth grade? You knew what you wanted to do in college in the sixth grade?"

"Yes."

"And I still don't have a clue."

"Not everyone knows what they want to do in college."

"Everyone I know has at least a small idea." He rolled onto his side and propped his head on his hand. "At least something they're good at. At the rate I'm going, I will graduate with a degree in pranking. I do a mean TP job. Can that go on a college application?"

"So you take generals until you figure out what you like."

"Isn't that basically what I'm doing now? Taking generals. And I like nothing."

I wasn't sure what to say to him. It was obvious he had been beating himself up over this for who knew how long. I rolled onto my side too and put my hand on his arm. "You'll figure it out."

"Everyone keeps telling me that, but what if I don't?"

This was his fear. I could see it in his eyes and I wished I could grab that Heath Hall mask and it could somehow work its magic on him too. But I knew it wasn't that simple. Nobody's fears were. Mine weren't. When tonight was over, I'd still have to figure out a way to face my parents.

"I know," he said, and rolled onto his back, my hand dropping into the space between us. "I'm not as fun when I'm serious." He jumped to his feet before I could tell him otherwise and quickly pulled me up to mine.

"Dance with me."

"What?"

"This is my favorite song."

The music was still in Spanish. I laughed as he pulled me into his arms and began swaying us to the beat.

"Really? Your favorite?"

"Yes. Listen."

For a second I thought he was serious. He sounded so serious. So I stopped talking and listened to the words . . . that I couldn't understand.

He gave a breathy laugh and I hit his chest, narrowing my eyes at him.

He continued to sway us and started singing quietly in English as though he were translating it for me. "Her stare can crash cars, fall trees, break hearts."

I tried to hold my narrow eyes, but I couldn't help but laugh.

"Her laugh can crash cars, fall trees . . ." He leaned in close, his lips next to my ear. "Break hearts."

I closed my eyes, tingles spreading down my spine as his breath touched my neck. Then my stomach growled loudly and he said, just as softly, "You think you could eat half a pie?"

I pulled back. "What?"

He released me from his arms. "Half a pie. Do you want to eat one?"

"Like a pizza or the fruit variety?"

"Are we from New York? Of course I mean a pie as in apple or pumpkin or berry."

"Do they still refer to pizzas as pies in New York or is that only in the movies?"

"I don't know, but this is a competition, Moore. Can you eat half a pie or can't you?"

"I can eat it faster than you, that's for sure."

"That's what I thought. I'm going to take you—well, have you take me—to the best place for pie that exists in this town at eleven o'clock at night. You can only get to

275

it by car, so it completely goes with the theme of your night."

"Okay, Holt. Let's go have a competition."

"Denny's?" I asked, staring at the sign.

"It's eleven o'clock at night. What did you expect, my grandma's kitchen?"

"I expected a secret location."

"Well, in twelve hours I can take you to a secret pie location, but this is the best I have right now."

We got out of the truck and walked to the glowing building. "Do you really know a secret pie location?"

"No, but I love that you thought I did."

"I didn't."

"You totally did."

The apple pie was at our table in ten minutes as most pies that have probably been sitting in the freezer for a couple days can be. Jackson cut the pie in half, being careful to measure it just right, then scooped one section onto his plate and another onto mine.

"That's a lot of pie."

"Are you already giving up?"

My stomach rumbled, and he laughed.

"Is it a timed event or are we just seeing who can eat the most?" I asked.

"Of course it's a timed event. Can you call something

an event if it isn't timed?" He picked up his fork.

"Oh, we get to use utensils?"

He raised his eyebrows. "You don't want to use utensils?"

"I do. I just thought you couldn't call something a pie-eating competition unless utensils weren't involved."

"Okay, crazy. No utensils." He put his fork down along with his phone, where he'd pulled up the timer app. "Ready?" he asked, raising his eyebrows at me.

I nodded.

"Go!"

He dug his face in the pie while I sat there and watched. I hadn't even been tempted to compete with him, which wasn't like me. Maybe things *were* happening tonight. Good things.

I wondered how long it would take before he realized I wasn't doing it. I picked up my fork and had a few bites. It was pretty good. I didn't think I could eat the whole thing anyway. That much sugar in one night after so many months off it would not feel good.

"Did you just prank me?" he asked after about ten seconds. His mouth was surrounded by pie filling. "That was good. I did not think you were going to do that. Now I look like an idiot."

"Isn't that your favorite?"

He picked up a chunk of pie with his hand and threw

it at me. It stuck in my hair.

"Gross." I was trying to get it out when he came around the table to my bench and went in for a hug.

I scooted back against the wall. "Don't you dare."

"I can't kiss you on the cheek?"

I picked up a napkin off the table and swiped it across his mouth. He took over the job, wiping his mouth clean, his eyes lit up in that happy way they did that made me warm inside.

"Can I take you somewhere?" I asked suddenly.

He looked at his phone. I did too. It was eleven thirty.

"You have to go. Never mind," I said. "Another night."

"You can take me somewhere. I can be a little late."

"Your parents won't get mad?"

"They might, but I'm willing to risk a possible grounding."

"I'll probably be grounded for the rest of my life anyway, so it's not like you'll get to go out anytime soon." I realized what I just said and amended it with, "I mean, with me. You can obviously go out with other people."

He gave me a lazy smile. "Let me pay the bill and clean up my face. I'll meet you in the truck in five."

THIRTY-TWO

I parked the truck in the dirt clearing and turned off the engine. The radio went off as well and the silence seemed loud in the cab.

"Where are we?"

He'd probably never come to the lake on this side. The lake wasn't even visible from where we'd parked. It was my secret little swimming cove. "Come here. I want to show you something." Before we got out, I pointed to the mask. "Maybe you should put that on."

He laughed. "I'm good."

"Wait, have you never worn it before?"

"Do you know how many people have worn that mask? The last girl who wore it was a little sketchy."

I hit his arm and he laughed.

"I don't believe you've never worn it."

"There's a process, a protocol. You have to get nominated and then approved by the keeper. I don't want to mess with the power of the mask, throw off the fine balance."

I shook my head and opened the door. "Come on."

He let me lead him down the dirt path that was so familiar to me. His hand felt nice in mine, like it belonged there. I stopped us at the edge of the path and turned off the light on my phone. Then I took him by the shoulders and faced him toward the lake that I knew was now less than ten steps away. The only thing I could see was a few bright spots in the darkness—the reflection of the stars above on the water. I positioned myself behind him, laying my cheek on his back. I wrapped my arms around him, placing one palm flat on his chest so I could feel his heartbeat.

He took a deep breath in.

"What do you see?" I asked.

"Nothing. Darkness."

"But you know there's something there, right?"

"I assume something is there."

"Just because you can't see the future, doesn't mean it doesn't exist. You don't have to see everything clearly or know exactly where you're going to move forward."

I slipped out of my shoes and whispered for him to do the same. I felt him shift as he stepped out of his.

"You move forward." I took a step, which pushed his leg forward and we walked like that until the water and mud seeped between our toes. "And when the future surrounds you, then you know where you are, what the steps you took led you to."

"Are we at the lake?" he asked. His voice was low and husky.

"I swim here sometimes. If I had a car, I could swim here a lot more." My cheek was still pressed up against his back, my arms still wrapped around his torso. Last time I had been here, I couldn't force myself to relax. Now my whole body seemed to lack muscles. It would melt to the ground if I let it. Jackson laid one of his hands on top of mine.

"Jackson?"

"Hmm?"

"I like you just as much when you're serious."

It surprised me when he took a shuddering breath.

"You owe me comfort through an emotional break-down," he said.

"Yes. I totally do."

At first I thought he was kidding, being funny, like he seemed to do when things got too heavy. But when he turned in my arms, put his forehead to my shoulder, and held on to me like his life depended on it, I realized he wasn't. I didn't think I was a sympathetic crier. I mean, my parents had cried many times and I'd stood there as dry eyed as the Sahara desert. But there was something about holding Jackson that got to me.

I rubbed his back like he had mine until it stilled. Until my feet were numb from the lake. He straightened up, touching his forehead to mine. He was a shadow in the darkness, but I could see his eyes shining. He took my face in his hands and kissed my cheeks where my tears lingered. Then he kissed my forehead. My hands held his wrists and I could tell he was going to move away so I tightened my hold. He paused, hesitated, then with a deep breath, kissed me.

My hands went to his hair, pulling him closer. His mouth was warm, his breath hot. I parted my lips and his tongue ran softly along them before it found mine, joining us closer together. He backed us out of the water, gripping my hips now. My hands went to his shoulders so that I didn't fall.

His mouth tasted of cinnamon. Cinnamon was my

new favorite flavor. My back hit a tree and he pressed himself against me.

And then his phone rang.

He groaned. "It must be twelve oh five."

I tried to catch my breath, unsuccessfully. "If it's your parents, you should answer so they know you're safe."

"I don't know that I *am* safe." He gave me a quick kiss, then picked up the phone.

I turned on my phone as well, shining the light on the ground so I could gather our shoes. I held them with one arm and with my other grabbed his hand and led him back to the truck while he assured whoever was on the phone that he was on his way home and had just lost track of time.

He hung up and kissed me again. "Yep. Totally worth it."

I smiled.

We both looked at our muddy feet. He opened the truck door, dug the squirt gun out of the Eric box, and sprayed my feet several times. "I thought that would work better," he said. "Like your brother was looking out for us or something."

"I'm guessing my brother would find this amusing."

"Are you once again pointing out that your brother is similar to me? After you were kissing me and everything?"

"Jackson. You are not my brother."

He squirted my feet one more time. "I think I would've liked your brother."

I hugged him. "I think I would've too."

THIRTY-THREE

I tried not to register the mud now on the floor mats. I'd clean them up later. I'd put everything back to normal later. It would all be fine.

"I think the seat belt over here is broken," he said, sliding next to me as I drove away from the lake and toward his house.

My heart seemed to stop. "It is? Can you fix it?"

"Moore, it was a joke. You know, the best pickup line ever."

"Oh. Right. It's just this truck: nothing can happen to it."

"I know. It's fine. You've done fine." He kissed my cheek.

"Don't distract me. I have to drive."

He rested his hand on my knee, which wasn't any less distracting. "Didn't we already hear this song? Is the radio playing repeats?"

He was right. We *had* heard it. Or at least the first part of it, not the whole thing.

"That happened last time we stopped too. Is it a . . ." He pushed a button and the music stopped and a tape came sliding out of the slot on top. "It's a tape."

My breath caught. "It is? It must've been his. Does it say anything on it?"

He took it out and flipped it once. "No. But someone made it. There are too many artists on it to be one album."

"Do you think Eric made it?"

"I don't know, but if he did, he had excellent taste in music."

"I was going to say the same thing."

He smiled and put the tape back in the player. "Thanks for letting me be part of tonight. I had fun."

"Me too. I guess you need to take Heath Hall away now." I nodded toward the dash where he and his empty eyes still gazed at us creepily.

He loaded him into the backpack and zipped it up. "Do you have anyone you want to nominate to wear this?"

"Besides you?"

"I just walked into an icy cold lake. I'm good."

I squeezed his hand. *Was* he good?

"I think I'm going to pass on the torch," he said. "Let someone else be the mask's keeper."

"Really?"

"I was hanging on to it for so long because I felt like it was the only purpose I had in my life. I think I was scared to let it go. But it's time for Heath to move on."

"Do you know who you're passing it to?"

"I'm not sure. What do you think about Amelia?"

The suggestion surprised me, but then it didn't. "She'd actually be pretty perfect."

We pulled up in front of his house and he didn't make any move to leave. Instead, he turned toward me. "I'm so proud of you. This"—he pointed to the floor of the truck—"was amazing. Best fear I've ever witnessed. You crushed it. Not that I'm surprised. That's what you do."

I wanted to feel good about his compliments, but dread was creeping its way into my shoulders, tightening them with each passing second. "It's not over yet."

"What are you going to do? About your parents? How

are you going to talk to them? Are you going to leave the truck for them to find?"

"No. Maybe. I have no idea."

"Someone once told me that you didn't need to know the future, you just had to move forward."

"Smart advice."

"I thought so."

"You should keep that person around in case they have other smart pieces of information to share." I had started the sentence as a joke but realized I was unsure of where we stood, what he wanted moving forward. Was this just a unique, rule-breaking night because of the mask and the challenge?

He pushed the hair back from my forehead, his eyes on mine. "I have to keep her around. She owns me." He kissed the corner of my mouth. "You own me."

I let out my breath and leaned into his kiss.

His phone rang again.

"It's like she knows." He laughed and answered it. "Mom, I'm home. I'm right outside just saying good night to Hadley."

Had he ever used my first name before? It sounded weird coming from him.

"More like forty-five minutes. And I'm here." He paused to listen to whatever she was saying. "Well, if

I'm already grounded for a week, then I'm just going to make out with her for ten more minutes."

I gasped. He put down his phone.

"You did not just say that to your mom."

"No, I didn't. She'd already hung up."

I grabbed a handful of the front of his shirt and pulled him toward me. I gave him a soft kiss.

"I thought you were going to hit me. This is way better." He kissed me twice more. "I better go, though. I wasn't kidding about the Mom-being-mad part."

"I know. Good luck with that."

"You too."

"Thank you."

He started to get out.

"Wait!" I called.

"What?"

"I need your phone number."

He laughed. "We did this way backward."

We switched phones and entered our numbers, then he left, throwing a smile over his shoulder as he did. A few minutes later my phone rang. Across my screen the words *My Hot Boyfriend calling* came on. I laughed and answered. "Hello."

"Do you agree?"

"About which part?"

"All of it."

"Yes." My cheeks hurt from the smile there. "Did you get in trouble?"

"Just a week. That's doable. Are you home yet?"

"No."

"Call me if you need me, after your parents get home," he said.

"Okay."

"Good night, Moore."

"Night."

THIRTY-FOUR

As I pulled up to my house, I expected sirens to sound, my parents to come rushing out yelling and screaming. But all was quiet, as I had left it. Everything was exactly the same. Not even Amelia's car was back. It was almost like it hadn't happened at all. Something should've been different to reflect how different I felt.

I sighed. Now I had to decide what to do with the truck. I had been planning on putting it back on the platform, but maybe I should leave it in the drive. It would force me to have the conversation with my parents that I'd been putting off practically my entire life.

My dad would be the first to see it the next night. It would shock him. Maybe even put him on the defense right away before I had a chance to share my feelings. Or maybe it would make him sad or scare him. I thought about every possible reaction my dad might have to seeing the truck, after eighteen years, not where it belonged. And regardless of how I felt, I didn't think that was fair to him. I couldn't go from saying nothing to doing the most dramatic thing possible. Both he and my mom deserved to be eased into what I needed to tell them. They didn't deserve a lightning strike.

I put the truck in park and got out. The ramps were where I left them in front of the platform so I moved them around to the back. Then ever so slowly, positioning the truck just right, I drove it forward. When I got to the top of the ramps, the truck stopped, not having enough power to get over the lip. I needed to give it more gas. I gripped the wheel and pressed gently on the gas pedal. It still wasn't enough. I'd gone up the ramps too slow. I thought about backing up and going up again, a little faster. First, I tried one last time with a little more pressure on the gas pedal. The truck lurched forward. I gasped and slammed on the brakes. It stopped just in time, inches from the front edge. I caught my breath.

Now I needed to back it up just a few inches. As I started to shift the truck in reverse, a set of headlights swept across the yard and a car pulled up to the front of the house. Amelia. Her eyes were wide as she climbed out of her car and saw me, the headlights of my brother's truck like a beacon across the lawn. I held up my finger, telling her to wait a minute, then looked over my right shoulder to back up. I lifted my foot off the brake pedal, but instead of moving backward, the truck jumped forward. The wheel jerked and the left front tire was off the platform and on the ground before I could step on the brake. The right tire was now suspended in midair in front of the ramp. I slid to the left, my body slamming into the door, my head hitting the window.

No. This couldn't be happening. I applied the gas, slowly trying to ease the truck forward, hoping to just get it all on the ground and start again. The left tire spun and spun, obviously not fully on the ground, which meant the platform must've been holding up some of the center of the truck. No.

Amelia knocked on the driver's-side window. I rolled it down with the cranking handle.

"What are you doing? Your parents are going to kill you."

"Not helping. How do I move it?"

She backed up, assessing the position of the truck. "One of the back wheels isn't fully grounded. You're stuck."

"Thanks. I caught that."

"Your parents are going to kill you."

"You already said that." I turned off the engine and opened the door. I fell out, barely catching myself before hitting the ground. Then I, too, backed up to assess the position of the truck. "What if I moved one of those ramps so it's facing backward under the left front tire and then drove forward a little?"

"Then what?" she asked.

"I don't know." I grabbed a fistful of my hair and a pain shot through my right shoulder. I pinched it hard. "Then put the other ramp forward under the right tire?"

"Then you'd just have this same situation but in reverse."

"You think?"

"I don't know. We can try it."

At two o'clock in the morning we gave up. The truck hadn't moved from its original lopsided position and I was pretty sure the only thing we'd managed to do was tear up a section of grass under the left tire. "It's fine. We'll fix this. We have all day tomorrow."

"Is it time to tell me yet what you were doing?"

"I was facing my fear. Being Heath Hall."

"What?"

I thought about telling her who and what Heath Hall

was and represented but I felt like that took away from the secrecy pact of it all. She'd know in a couple days when that backpack and instructions ended up in her care. So instead, I said, "My parents choose my brother over me every time."

She didn't argue. "I'm sorry."

"I'm tired of it. I thought if I drove this truck tonight that I'd be facing a fear, the fear of competing with his memories my whole life. I thought I'd be facing the memory of my dead brother once and for all. Telling him in a way that I had won. Or maybe that it shouldn't be a competition at all. I don't know. It sounds weird, I know."

"So wait, you drove this truck around? Like out of this yard?"

"Yes, I was just getting back when you pulled up."

"Wow, Hadley. And how did it feel?"

"Freeing."

She smiled. "I bet." She put her hands on her hips and looked at the truck again. "And now you're trying to put it back?"

"Yes."

She hesitantly asked, "What about your parents? Don't you want them to know?"

"I think the message would be a little too shocking. I want to ease them into it a bit by talking to them first."

"Probably a good idea . . . except." She gestured to the truck. "Now you'll just give them a heart attack."

"I know." I let out a defeated breath of air. "This will not go over well. It would've been one thing if I had just left it parked in the driveway. That would've been shocking enough. But this?" I couldn't even finish that thought out loud. This would be like a punch to the gut. This looked like a broken truck. A wrecked truck. This would be more than a shock. I felt beyond terrible. That's why I was going to fix this. I had to.

Amelia walked around the platform again, as though some new idea on how to solve this would suddenly come to her after over an hour of trying to figure something out and failing. "Where did you go?"

"All the places I wanted to go and never could. I took Jackson."

She clapped and gave a little jump. "Tell me everything."

I climbed up on the platform and into the bed of the truck. It teetered just a bit with my weight but the way it was sloped forward provided a really good angle to sit. I patted a space next to me.

She raised her eyebrows. "Are you sure? I've never been inside his truck before."

"Neither had I. Come on. Let's talk. I want to hear all about your night with DJ as well."

She joined me, then laid her head on my shoulder. "You have no idea how proud I am of you right now."

I gave a single laugh. "For what? For taking my brother's truck and failing to put it back right?"

"No. For realizing that you don't have to earn your parents' love." She squeezed my hand. "And if they don't kill you first, I'm sure they'll realize that too."

"Thanks. Very helpful."

"Maybe Jackson will know how to right this truck. We should call him."

"At two o'clock in the morning? I think I can wait until a decent hour. My dad won't be home until tonight anyway. I have time."

Amelia stretched and leaned her head back to look at the sky. "This is a great view."

I looked up as well. The stars were bright tonight. "How long have you known that my swimming was about my parents? My brother?"

"First of all, you love swimming. Don't let this make you think you don't. But in a race, as soon as you tap the wall, your gaze goes first to the scoreboard. If, and only if, your name is in the top spot, do you look to the stands." She took my hand in hers. "Maybe now you can swim for yourself, Hadley. Enjoy it even more."

THIRTY-FIVE

I awoke with a pain in my neck and two mosquito bites on my right arm. A bird chirped from the tree above. I groaned and rubbed at my neck while I sat up. The hard metal floor of the truck bed was not a comfortable mattress.

My phone, sitting next to me, informed me it was only seven a.m. The sun or the bird or the mosquito bites must've woken me up because this was too early to get up on a Saturday morning. Amelia still slept next to me, hugging a pillow, the blankets pulled up over her ears. The night slowly came back to me: taking the keys, driving my brother's truck off the ramp, getting my brother's truck stuck on the platform, then spending hours talking to Amelia in the back of it. At some point during the night, I had run inside, grabbed some blankets and pillows because we were cold, and brought them back out to the truck so we could finish talking. We must've fallen asleep.

My head ached. The events of last night did not seem better this morning. The sun only made everything that much clearer. The huge patch of grass stripped away, now muddy and dark beneath the front tire, looked so much worse in the light of the day. I let out a small whine.

I carefully climbed out of the truck and walked around it once. What I needed was some leverage, something to pull it off the platform. If my dad's truck were here, we could use it. But it wasn't. Who else had a truck?

I knew Jackson would still be asleep, plus he was grounded, but I sent off a text anyway so that the second he woke up he might be able to help. Maybe he knew someone. This would be fixed today. I had about eleven hours. We could right this in eleven hours.

So . . . do you know anyone with a big truck?

My text probably woke him up because minutes later he replied. Why?

I answered: Let's say, hypothetically, of course, a truck you were trying to put back on a platform was now stuck lopsided on said platform.

I'd text my hot boyfriend so he would come over and help me.

You have a hot boyfriend too? Unfortunately, mine is grounded so he can't help me. Do you think yours can help me?

Funny. So are you just messing with me to be funny or is this hypothetical situation a sad reality?

Yes to the second option.

That sucks. I'll be over in a minute.

You're grounded.

I'll ask my mom. She forgets everything when she's sleeping.

Amelia sat up in the bed of the truck and stretched with a loud sigh. I tucked my phone into my pocket.

"Hey," I said. "Your parents have a truck."

"Yes, it pulls the trailer with Cooper's quads."

"Do you think they would let Cooper borrow it to come help us?"

"Of course. I'll call him."

By the time Jackson arrived ten minutes later, my hair and teeth were brushed and Amelia and I were sitting up in the truck bed watching him walk the path to us.

"He's cute," Amelia said. "Even when it looks like he just rolled out of bed."

He was wearing the same sweats from the night before but with a green T-shirt that I was sure would make his eyes look amazing once he was close enough for me to see them. His hair was a curly mess on top of his head and I could still see some mud streaks around his ankles from our time at the lake last night. I looked at my ankles and realized I sported the same streaks.

He had on a lazy smile and my heart constricted in my chest.

"Wow, Moore, you did this all by yourself?"

"Shut up. We have a plan."

He did a full loop around the truck. Then another. "What's the plan?"

Amelia raised her hand. "A big truck and a rope."

"So I take it you don't want to tell your parents, then?" he asked me.

"I do," I said, meeting his eyes so he could see the sincerity in mine. "I just don't want this to be the first thing they see."

He nodded. "I understand."

Amelia hopped down from the truck. "I am going to get us donuts before Cooper gets here. I sense this is going to be a long morning."

Amelia walked to her car parked on the street, then climbed in and drove away. The second her car rounded the corner Jackson said, "Are you going to come give me a hug or do I have to come up there?"

My cheeks went warm. "I wasn't sure if . . ."

"If what? Did you not tell Amelia about us yet?"

"No. I told her."

"You did?"

"Should I not have?"

In three big steps he was up on the platform and in the bed of the truck with me. I let out a yelp of surprise but then threw my arms around him.

"I thought I'd wake up this morning and find out you put the truck back perfectly in its place and wanted to not only pretend you hadn't driven it, but pretend nothing had happened at all." He interlaced our fingers together and leaned up against the side.

"When I came home last night everything looked eerily perfect at my house. Exactly the same and it felt so wrong. This mess I've made is a nightmare but at least it represents how different my life feels now."

"Are you scared?"

"Terrified."

He kissed me then, bringing our linked hands behind his back, pulling me closer to him. He tasted like toothpaste and pulled away too fast.

"I don't know how long I can stay before my mom wakes up and remembers she grounded me last night."

My eyes were still closed from the kiss. "You don't have to go yet."

He gave a breathy laugh, then his lips were back on

mine. The truck tipped a little, not fully balanced on its perch. I let out a gasp and Jackson pulled back.

"Is it going to fall?" he asked.

"No. Amelia and I tried all sorts of counterweight maneuvers on it last night to get some traction. It's pretty much wedged here. It's just teasing us."

His eyes turned worried. "You okay?"

"I'm fine."

"Worse-case scenarios?"

My shoulders tensed up and I cringed. "Let's not think about those right now. Let's just fix this."

"What's wrong?"

"Nothing," I started to say, but then said, "My shoulders. I haven't swum in a while. They're stiff."

He moved his hands to my shoulders and began rubbing them. "Do you think that maybe your shoulder pain has less to do with swimming and more to do with stress?"

"There does seem to be a correlation."

"Maybe instead of working on conditioning them, you need to work on de-stressing your life."

I laughed. "I'm trying." I patted the edge of the truck. "This isn't exactly the most relaxing situation."

"We'll fix it," he said.

"We have to."

THIRTY-SIX

Cooper's truck rumbled up the drive.

"Cooper's here!" Amelia called, shoving the rest of the donut into her mouth and running toward the drive.

"Oh," Abby said as she climbed from the passenger side. "Fun."

"So much fun," I said dryly. "Did Cooper bring a rope or do I need to find one in the garage?"

"He brought one." Abby turned to Jackson. "Hi, I'm Abby."

"I'm Jackson. The boyfriend."

I smiled with that statement.

Cooper joined us, putting an arm around Abby's waist. "You ready to save this beautiful truck?"

"Yes, please," I said.

As Cooper and I studied the bumper and wrapped the rope, I heard Jackson say to Abby, "So I heard you've met the guy who plays Heath Hall in the movies. Grant James."

"Who told you that?" I asked.

Amelia laughed. "You know I tell that to everyone with ears."

Abby smiled. "Me too. And yes I have. He starred in a movie with one of my best friends: Lacey Barnes."

"Wait, you know Lacey Barnes?" Jackson asked. "That's what you should be bragging about, Amelia."

"How is Lacey doing, anyway?" Amelia asked.

"Great. She's working on another movie and still dating Donavan Lake."

"Is he famous too?" Jackson asked.

"No, but he's great."

"I think this will work," Cooper said, tugging on the rope and bringing my attention back to the task. "Just let me back up the truck."

"Sounds good."

I clutched the steering wheel, ready to direct the truck the right way as soon as it was free of the platform.

Amelia, Abby, and Jackson stood off to the side, Jackson chomping on his second donut and Amelia laughing at something he said as they waited for the show to start. Cooper revved the engine. My heart was in my throat. I turned on the music to drown out the sounds of my own breathing that was making me even more nervous. Jackson gave me a thumbs-up—to show support or to show his approval for the Pearl Jam song that now blasted out of the speakers, I wasn't sure. Or maybe he was giving the go ahead to Cooper because suddenly his truck lurched forward, my cue to give a little gas as well.

The rope tied between the two trucks snapped taut and vibrated with the new tension. My brother's truck moved forward ever so slowly. At first my whole body relaxed with the motion until a sound so loud I could hear it over the scream of the music—a groaning, a screeching of metal—pierced the air. The underside of the truck was being dragged along the edge of the platform. My first instinct was to slam on the brakes, not wanting to damage the truck. Cooper either didn't hear the sound or didn't have the same instinct because he kept moving forward. That's when two other sounds happened almost simultaneously: first a loud creak, then a bang as the entire platform bent to one side, then collapsed. I bounced in the seat as the truck slammed onto the ground, all four tires finally level. The second sound was a ripping of metal as the front bumper of my brother's truck was ripped free, flying through the air, and hitting the back of Cooper's truck, then falling to the ground. That's when his brake lights flashed and he finally stopped moving forward.

Pressure pushed against my ears, muffling the sound of the music as I stared at that unassuming piece of metal on the ground in front of me. A piece of metal that was sure to ruin my life. This was not supposed to happen. I was supposed to fix this, not shock my parents. And definitely not break my brother's priceless truck.

Nobody moved. It felt like time had slowed down. The hope of hiding all of this vanished. What had I done?

Images of my parents' reactions flew through my mind in still frames, each one worse than the last. The final image, the one that stayed as if trying to burn its likeness into my vision was my mom, her arms folded, wearing the face I had seen so often lately: disappointment. No matter what I did, how hard I worked, I could never escape that face. Now it would follow me for the rest of my life.

Something snapped in me. Despite what I'd been saying about how I had changed and I wanted things to be different, until that moment, I had hoped they could at least be close to how they were before. But nothing could be the same after this. Anger coursed through me, anger that had been resting just beneath the surface for a long time.

I tugged open the door and stalked toward the bumper. The music poured out of the open cab behind me, my soundtrack to a breakdown. I thought I heard my name but my ears still felt blocked, pulsing with the sound of rushing blood. Even as I told myself I was overreacting, even as I tried to calm my beating heart, I couldn't stop myself. I picked up the bumper. It was heavier than it looked and threw me off balance for a moment. I stumbled forward but then righted myself. I lifted it over my head, my shoulders protesting with a sharp pain ripping through them. I ignored the warning and hurled the bumper with all my might to the ground. It kicked up a few rocks but skidded to a halt, its leash still attached to Cooper's truck. I picked it up again by one end and hit it over and over again onto the driveway. Each strike left a black mark on the white pavement. And each strike mangled the bumper a little more. As I was about to lift the bumper again, a crackling voice came out of the cab of Eric's truck behind me.

"Those are the songs that make me feel alive. Although, if you're listening to this now, it's probably because I'm dead. In which case, I hope you played at least one of those songs at my funeral. If you didn't, go dance on my grave to one of them. I know, Mom, too morbid. But if you can't laugh, what's life worth?" His voice was so familiar, a bit like my dad's, and yet so foreign.

I couldn't catch my breath. It came in rapid short bursts that weren't filling my lungs like they needed to be filled. My shoulders hurt so bad I was sure I had torn something.

My eyes darted to the bent and battered bumper. A pair of arms wrapped around me from behind. The smell of flowers enveloped me. Amelia. "You're okay," she whispered. "You're going to be okay."

Jackson was on the ground untying the bumper from the rope.

Cooper was out of his truck, eyes wide. "I'm sorry, I thought that ring was anchored to the frame." He was pointing at a piece on the back side of the bumper. "I hadn't meant for the bumper to handle all that pressure."

"Can we fix it?" Jackson asked, freeing the bumper and analyzing the damage. "We can rebuild the platform, right?"

Cooper's eyes went to the collapsed platform still beneath the truck behind them.

Abby was walking around it now. "The supports are just bent. If we unscrew them and pound them out . . ."

"No," I said.

Everyone went still and looked at me.

"No. We can't hide this. It's done." I had done this and

now I'd have to face my parents. The air was quiet, no more music was playing and no other hidden messages from my brother.

"What do you need us to do?" Amelia asked.

"Nothing. I wanted to talk to my parents. This is good. I just need some time alone if that's okay." I needed to think and to stand under hot water, then ice my aching shoulders.

"Are you sure?" Amelia asked. "I don't want to leave you alone like this."

Like this. Like the mess that I had become. The girl who could beat her brother's bumper to twisted scrap metal. The girl who was obviously unstable. "Check in on me if you need to but I'm fine. I promise. I need to prepare myself. I need some space to think."

Amelia nodded and went to the house, probably to gather her things.

Cooper gave me an apologetic shrug. "Sorry about . . ." He looked at the bumper, at the platform, then back to me.

"It's okay. Thanks for trying."

Abby gave me a small wave and she and Cooper climbed into their truck and left.

Then it was just me and Jackson. I couldn't even look at him. He probably thought I was crazy. I felt a little crazy.

As if reading my mind, he said, "It's about time you lost it."

My eyes snapped to his and he had on his trademark smile. The one that made it look like life was just a joke waiting to be told.

"I told you a long time ago to run as far from me as possible, didn't I?"

"And to think if I had I would've missed this awesome display." He nudged the bumper with his toe.

"Apparently, I have to be the best at breakdowns as well."

He laughed. "I was thinking the same thing. Show-off."

I smiled as well but then took a deep breath. "Jackson, I—"

"You can't get rid of me that easily," he said before I could finish. "Come on, I'll help you clean things up."

He stepped toward me but I stopped him with, "I just need time. To think."

He looked hurt and that confused me.

"You need your earphones?" he asked.

"What?" It took me another second to realize that he was upset because he thought I needed time to think about him, about us, when I really just meant I needed to think about the night in front of me with my dad. And how I was going to clean up the mess I'd made. I was about to say as much when he put on his smile that closed him off, protected him.

I started to panic. Why was he pulling away?

"That's what you do, right?" he asked. "Shut out the world when things get real. I thought you had some sort of breakthrough. That you realized that closing yourself off to everyone and climbing inside your head, living in the past, didn't help. That you realized you need other people."

My defenses shot up with his attack. I didn't need him telling me how to deal with my problems and I definitely didn't need him telling me everything I'd been doing wrong. I'd already had a guy willing to do that. "When did I say any of that?"

"I don't know, maybe when you showed up on my porch last night. When you texted me this morning."

"I asked for a little space, Jackson. Is that so wrong? What do you want from me?"

"Nothing, Hadley." And with that he walked away. I didn't move as he started his car. I didn't move as he drove away.

"What just happened?" Amelia asked, her backpack on her shoulder, her shoes in her hand.

"I think he's done with me."

"No, he's not. He's just upset that you don't need him to stay."

I wondered if she was projecting. If she was the one upset.

"He'll be fine tomorrow," she said. "He'll understand. You just need some downtime. You're kind of in a big mess right now."

She understood. I nodded.

"Are you sure you don't want me to stay?"

Jackson was wrong, I *had* learned that I needed other people. But I had also learned that some things had to be faced alone. "I'm sure."

"Call me if you need me."

THIRTY-SEVEN

rewound the tape and listened to those six sentences . . . for the tenth time. There was a smile in Eric's voice as he spoke and I couldn't help but agree with my dad. His tone, his making something serious into a joke seemed very much like Jackson.

I'd put the mangled bumper in the bed of the truck and moved the truck to the driveway. I'd tried to move the platform that was now bent and broken, but it was too heavy. The torn-up grass I'd pieced back together the best I could, covering the major bald spot, but it was a muddy mess even when I was done. Inside the truck,

I'd cleaned the floor mats, wiped down the seats, and even refilled the water gun. I'd showered until the hot water ran cold and now I sat in the cab, ice packs on my shoulders, listening to his voice over and over. My parents had some home videos of my brother from when he was younger, cancer free. But none from when he was older. So this was the first time I'd heard his mature voice.

After he spoke, there was twenty minutes' worth of silence. I knew this because I listened to every second of the rest of the tape to make sure he hadn't said anything else. Then I rewound the tape all the way to the beginning and played the whole thing again, taking note of the songs now that I knew what they represented—songs that made him feel alive.

It was late in the afternoon by the time I finally pulled myself from the cab and went inside. I hung the keys to the truck carefully back in their glass box in the kitchen. Not that it would help. My parents would still know I had taken them out. My phone had died an hour before so I plugged it in.

Three missed calls were waiting for me when it got some charge back. All from my mother. Did she know? Had my neighbor called and tattled? There was no way someone hadn't seen what was going on this morning.

As I was contemplating whether to call her back or

not, my phone rang again, her name flashing on the screen. I took a deep breath and answered.

"Hello."

"Hadley, hi. I've been trying to call you."

"My phone was dead. Is the race done?" Maybe if we talked about that first, she'd know I was still a good daughter.

"It finished a couple hours ago."

"It went smoothly?"

"Very. I was going to stay until tomorrow, but I'm tired and your father is coming home tonight and I just want to have all day tomorrow with the two of you. I need some family time. So I'm already on my way home. I should be there by nine."

Family time? *Now* she wanted family time?

"And Dad?" I so needed my dad to be home first. He would help me explain this all to Mom. He would make it better.

"I think he'll be home closer to ten."

I swallowed. When the lump in my throat didn't budge, I swallowed again. "Okay." It wasn't too late to run away. My grandparents might take me.

"How was your weekend?" she asked. "Fun?"

I might as well prepare her now. "Interesting. I need to tell you something when you get home."

"Did you throw a party?" she asked, laughing like she

knew it wasn't a possibility.

"No."

"What is it, then?"

"I'd rather not talk about it over the phone."

"Okay, we'll talk when I get home, then. Love you."

"Love you too." I was glad we'd said it now because it might not be said for a long time after today.

My first instinct when I hung up was to get onto my computer and talk to the guy who'd been giving me advice for over a month now. It took me two seconds to remember that guy was also the one who just walked away from me like he was finished. No, he wasn't finished. He was just hurt that I didn't want him to stay, like Amelia said. Everything would be fine once we talked again.

I signed onto the computer anyway, thinking I could just read over our old conversations and get something helpful out of them. But they were gone. Every last private message we'd shared had been deleted. And since I hadn't done it, that meant Jackson had. My heart tightened in pain and I quickly shut the computer. If I hadn't thought he was walking away before, I knew now. He was done with me. Just like that.

The next five hours went by both painfully slow and alarmingly fast. I spent them cleaning. Icing my shoulders more. Making sure everything was in order so that when Mom came home, at least she'd be happy about one thing. I wasn't sure if I should wait outside, sitting on the tailgate of the truck. Or if I should let her have her reaction in private and wait inside, where hopefully she'd have concealed some of the initial shock.

Like the coward I decidedly was, I chose inside.

I wore my hair down and put on a nice outfit, as though I were waiting for a date. I was usually in swim gear so this, too, would make my mom happy.

The key in the lock sent my heart racing. I began a silent plea, to God or to my brother or to whoever was listening, that this wouldn't break apart my family. The sound of things, her purse maybe, hitting the entryway floor, followed by rushing feet prepared me for her arrival. And then there she was, standing in the doorway to the living room, a panicked look on her face.

When she saw me, that panicked look melted into relief. I was confused by the reaction but then anger took over her features. That's what I'd been expecting.

"I'm sorry," I choked out. "I didn't mean to."

"What. Happened."

The speech I had rehearsed for five hours left me faster than I could blink. It was a good speech, if I remembered. One that explained how sorry I was and how much I just wanted to feel equally loved. Something that would make me sound apologetic and her feel guilty. That had seemed like the right balance. But my brother's voice on the tape was repeating over and over in my head. *If you can't laugh, what's life worth?*

And that's when I saw the humor in the last few days. Eric would've found it all funny, I was sure of it. Me stealing his stupid truck. Heath Hall mask on the dash. Jackson squirting me. Slurpees and muddy feet and kissing. And last of all, me unable to put it all back together, sleeping in the truck bed, prying off the bumper. It was all very funny. I'd had an adventure with my brother, in a way, and I wasn't sorry for it. I was happy about it. It wasn't a good time to laugh and I was sure half the reason for this reaction was sheer exhaustion but I couldn't help it. I laughed.

THIRTY-EIGHT

Mom was so good at the disappointed face. Like she had practiced it in front of the mirror hundreds of times to make it just perfect. I had just gotten my laughter under control when she pulled out the face and that thought sent me laughing again.

"Are you on something? Have you been drinking?" she asked.

I was never going to stop laughing if she kept saying stuff like that. I tried to think of something sobering. Death. My brother's death. But again, that only made me smile as I thought about dancing on his grave. He *was* morbid.

I had come up with a five-minute speech that I was going to have to cut to five seconds because of my hysterics. "I took his truck. I was mad at you for missing my award ceremony and I couldn't tell you that."

"So you took your anger toward me out on your brother's truck?"

Her anger was the perfect medicine for my laughter. It stopped immediately. It stopped because she didn't have the right to be angry. I did. I got to be mad about this not her. "Yes, actually."

That surprised her. I could tell because she stuttered at first, unsure of what to say. "Well, that's . . . you . . . there will be consequences for this."

I thought about my shoulders, pretty sure there already were consequences for this. That thought made me even angrier. Was my swimming career over? Had I damaged them permanently this time? I stood and went to my bedroom.

"Don't walk away from me!" she yelled after me.

I retrieved the award from beneath my bed, went back, and dropped the envelope at her feet. "That's the last one of those I'll probably get. I'm glad you wanted to see me win it."

Her anger seemed to fade as she stared at the envelope. Finally, she bent down and picked it up. "What is this?" she asked after she took it out.

The small square showing the distinction was missing so I took the envelope from her, dug it out, then handed it to her.

She scanned the words.

I sat back on the couch, my anger fading as well. "I really didn't mean to break the truck. I was just going to drive it. Face my fear of him, of you always choosing him. And then I was going to put it back. But it all went wrong."

She sat down in the chair by the couch as though she couldn't stand anymore. "What do you mean me always choosing him?"

I had finally controlled my emotions. "Mom, you know what I mean. You have to."

"But it's not him I'm choosing. This is what I do. This is my job now. People count on me. I go to all your swim meets. I went to all your grade school sporting events." She stopped, her gaze going back to the award still in her hands. She took a deep breath. "I chose him over you." A single tear fell down her cheek and she swiped it away. Then she put the award on the end table next to her and looked at me for several long minutes. But she wasn't looking at me; she was looking through me, lost in her thoughts. "My grief has become a living thing."

"I know," I said. Because I really did know. I knew what this was. I knew she hadn't gotten over my brother's death.

"I've fed that grief year after year. I let it grow. I have let it take over my life." She put her face in her hands. "I have let it take over *our* lives. Hadley, my sweet girl, I'm sorry."

I opened, then closed my mouth again. Of all the reactions I was expecting, it wasn't this. I didn't expect her to recognize it so quickly.

She wiped at her tears again and met my eyes. "When I came home and saw the platform bent, saw the truck in the drive, I thought . . . I thought someone had tried to steal it. I thought someone had come into our house. Had hurt you. I was so scared."

Maybe the disaster outside with the truck had helped her come to these realizations more quickly than she might have otherwise. "You weren't worried about the truck?"

"I was worried about you. I love you. You know that, right?"

I nodded. I did know that. Things just needed to be different.

"I never saw anyone after I lost him. A professional, I mean. Someone to help me through my grief. We had you and you brought so much joy into our lives and I pushed that grief of losing him deep down. I thought I'd moved forward. I hadn't."

I stood. "Can I show you something?"

She let me get the keys and lead her out to the truck. She climbed inside with me and reverently touched the dash like she hadn't been inside since he was alive. I turned on the engine and played the recording of Eric.

Sobs shook her shoulders as she listened.

Yes, it was decided. I was definitely a sympathetic crier.

When it got to the part about laughing, my mom smiled through her tears. "I don't believe this has been in here this whole time."

"He sounds fun."

"He *was* fun."

The sound of the tape turning in the deck made me reach forward and turn it off.

"And moody and angry and belligerent sometimes," she said.

I looked at my mom in surprise.

"It's easier to remember the good times." She tapped the lid of the cardboard box that sat between us filled with the memories of Eric.

"What would you put in a box like that for me?" I asked, and wished I hadn't because *that* seemed morbid, that seemed unfair, and I had put her on the spot.

But she didn't seem to mind. She smiled. "Lots of swim stuff for sure, caps and goggles and swimsuits."

That was the easy answer but I was glad she'd been able to think of something so fast.

"And music," she went on. "You've always loved music. From the time you were little. It seems to take you to another place."

"I like music."

"I know. And we can't forget your lime Slurpees. Those would go in there. Plus, your phone. And probably a best friend charm to represent what a wonderful friendship you have with Amelia. You truly are an amazing friend. Loyal and giving."

I wasn't sure if she was going on and on because she felt so guilty or if she just couldn't stop herself but I didn't care either way. I was happy.

"I'd have to bottle some sand from the lake because you're always there in the summer. And maybe one of your many ribbons to show how competitive you are."

"Okay, Mom," I said, thinking that maybe she'd go on all night if I let her.

"I'm sorry for ever making you feel like I didn't know all that." So she did realize why I needed to hear it. "Sometimes, Hadley, I think that you don't need me. You're so independent. So hardworking and motivated and dedicated. And I feel like you have your life all figured out and that you don't need me for a thing. I should've never let that feeling be my excuse."

The words Jackson said earlier about how I shut people out came flying back into my mind. "I need you," I told my mom. "I'll always need you."

"Good." She kissed my forehead and gave me a hug. "Because I'll always need you too."

When she let me go, I pulled the squirt gun out of the cardboard box and pointed it at her. "What do you say? You want to go dance on a grave?" I squirted her.

She held up her hands with a squeal. "Yes. Let's."

I started to get out.

She touched my shoulder, stopping me. "Let's take this truck."

This truck. Had she ever referred to it as "this" anything in her life? It had always been Eric's truck. I wasn't sure I wanted it to be mine. I kind of wanted something that didn't make me a little bit sad every time I looked at it. But it was nice that it was possibly an option now.

I nodded and took a deep breath. Just as we were about to back out of the driveway, my dad pulled up.

"Is he going to kill me?" I asked, nearly forgetting I had another parent to talk through this.

She threw the door open, slid the box to the floor,

and shifted to the seat next to me. "Daniel, we're going for a dance."

My dad approached the truck, wary. He took in the collapsed platform and the bumper I'd thrown into the back. His normal smile was far from present. "What's going on?" he asked in a heavy voice. One which showed that when he offered to sell this truck, he might not have been quite emotionally ready.

Mom patted the seat next to her. "Hop in. I'll explain on the way."

She would explain on the way. I didn't have to. This brought me a lot of relief. He sat down next to her, still in his work suit, his tie loosened. She started with, "Your daughter won a swim award a couple weeks ago that usually only seniors win."

My dad chuckled a bit as he shut the door. "I'm not surprised." He reached behind my mom and squeezed my shoulder. I winced but gritted through the pain.

"Congratulations," he said.

"Thanks."

Then my mom told him everything we'd talked about and finished by playing him the tape. He smiled through tears. Then we went and played Eric's music loudly while we visited his grave in the dark.

As we walked back to the truck, my dad ahead of us,

I looked at my mom and said, "You know I don't expect you to just stop doing all your charity work, right? I know that makes you happy."

"I know. But I need to find a balance. A healthy balance. I'll work on it. I promise."

"Me too." Because I needed a healthy balance as well. Robert had been right. I had been too focused on one thing. But he didn't know why. Jackson had figured that out. I was competing. Competing with my dead brother. Now I needed to learn to swim for me. I touched my shoulder. If that was still a possibility.

My dad slowed until he was walking beside me and draped his arm around my neck. "Should we go get some Froyo?"

"Yes," both my mom and I said together.

THIRTY-NINE

Amelia had checked on me approximately fifty times since Saturday. Every message some variation of the words *You good?*

It's like she thought my parents had stolen my phone and were answering texts while I rotted in the basement as punishment for what I'd done. I didn't blame her. I thought I'd be in bigger trouble too. I did get a stern lecture about taking the truck without asking and my dad told me I had to visit several junkyards to help him find a replacement bumper. We had talked as a family and were still trying to decide what to do with the truck.

My mom was all for me driving it. My dad thought we should sell it and I kept flipping back and forth between the two. I wanted to take my time. I didn't want to sell it and regret it later. For now, I decided to continue riding to school with Amelia and use it only when I really needed to go somewhere . . . like to get an apple pie.

Without Jackson, apparently. I hadn't heard from him since our fight. I'd thought about reaching out to him, but along with being sad about what had happened between us, I found myself angry. Angry at how he had acted. At how he'd made everything about him on the hardest day of my life.

My shoulders were still bothering me and that terrified me. I couldn't lose swimming over this too. For that I decided to take a long break. My mom was going to take me to the doctor the following week. But there was no harm in a break. At least that's what I told myself over and over.

Amelia pulled up to my house Monday morning and took in the now-empty spot where the truck used to be. My dad had hauled away the platform Sunday. The grass beneath it was dead. I climbed in her car.

"You good?" she asked.

I smiled. "For the fifty-first time, yes, I'm good."

"Why are you not grounded for twenty years?"

"Guilt."

She laughed. "Ah. You get the guilt-parenting? How have you worked this to your advantage?"

"I didn't get grounded." I hoped I'd find a new normal soon with my parents because as much as I didn't want to be in trouble, I didn't want them to feel guilty forever and it seemed like that was going to be the case for a while. They were walking on eggshells around me and it wasn't good.

"Oh, Hadley, come on. Years of neglect. You need to collect the guilt-parenting perks while they last. They'll be gone soon."

I shoved her arm.

"How are you and Jackson?"

My heart clenched. "I don't want to talk about it."

"He hasn't called begging for forgiveness?"

"No." He'd erased every trace of me from his life. He'd walked away. He was done.

"I'm sorry."

"It's okay." But I wasn't sure it was.

Amelia and I walked our separate ways to first period. I needed to drop by my locker and pick up a book. My locker was outside the B building, fourth row down. Today the row was fairly empty. A blond girl at the end was piling books from her backpack into her locker. She gave me a smile as she exited. I turned the dial on my lock and opened the door. A clear plastic cup sat inside, its bright green contents immediately making my mouth water.

"You're still on sugar, yes?" a voice from above me said, and I yelped, nearly dropping the Slurpee. I backed up, until I bumped into the row of lockers behind me, and looked up. Sitting on top of the lockers was Heath Hall.

"You were right." He tugged at the neck of the mask with his right hand. "This thing *is* hot." In his left hand he held a Slurpee. He took a sip through the small hole that made up the mouth on the mask. "It's a good thing I have a favorite drink that is nice and cold."

My fear dissolved but was replaced with the anger that had been competing for space the last couple days. I'd had a really hard weekend and he hadn't even checked on me. Instead, he'd walked away and now was making a joke out of what I assumed was his apology.

"Someone once told me that all good apologies are accompanied by a bribe." He gestured toward the Slurpee I held. I stepped forward, retrieved my math book out of the locker, and shut the door. "How did you get this in my locker?"

"I have a few people on staff that like me as well."

I narrowed my eyes. "Ms. Lin?"

"I hear she's your mentor. Knows all about your inner

artist. And gets to keep locker combinations in case her poor students forget them."

"And apparently she gives them out to anyone who asks."

"Don't be mad at her. Who can resist this charm?" He took another drink. "This is still really gross." He set it next to him. "Is everything good with your parents?" he asked.

"We're going to chat about my parents with you on top of the lockers?"

"Yes."

The late bell rang and I turned to leave. He jumped down, cutting me off before I could walk away. He grabbed my hand.

I pulled it free. "Is this really how we're going to do this? You're going to show up here misusing the mask and assume I'm going to get over it just because you're trying to be funny?"

"I'm not misusing the mask. This is my fear."

"No, this is you being ridiculous. You faced your fear out at the lake."

"I thought I did. But then something occurred to me this weekend. I thought my fear was just about me not knowing what I want. And that's definitely part of it. But my main problem is that I don't commit fully. To anything. To a future. To my schoolwork. To a girl."

I met his eyes. They were all I could see of him. "Will you take that ridiculous thing off? I can't take you seriously with it on."

"Are you saying you can take me seriously with it off?"

"Good point."

He glanced around, probably making sure the row was still empty, and took off the mask. His expression wasn't one of humor like I'd expected. He actually looked serious and sad, like he really had been agonizing over this all weekend. His hair was even messier than usual and I kept myself from running my fingers through it. He stared at the mask for a long moment.

"I couldn't even put this thing on at the lake to face my fear. It's like I couldn't even commit to that fear. And even when I do know what I want . . ." He looked at me then. "I'm scared to grab hold of it. I'm scared to say it's what I want just in case I end up being wrong. So on Saturday, with you, I left at the first sign that you might've been calling us off. I acted like it was you throwing walls up when really it was me. As soon as I got home, I knew I'd made a mistake, that I shouldn't have been a jerk. That your request for space wasn't about me." He held up the mask. "This is me saying I'm done being scared.

This is me committing to my fears, to my life, to you. I'm holding on to you if you'll have me."

I stared at the mask in his hand, at the drink in mine, then looked up at him again. "If this is how you realized you felt this weekend, why didn't you call me? Text me? Come over?"

"Because one, you asked for space and I was trying to respect that. And two, I got my phone taken away for leaving Saturday morning when I was supposed to be grounded. The only time I could've snuck over to your house was after my parents were asleep and I figured you were in big trouble so I didn't want to make it worse. I've been worried about you all weekend."

It all made sense. But something still didn't sit right. The thing that had made me think he was walking away for good. "Why did you erase all our chats?"

"What . . . ?" He looked at me, confused for a moment, then realization came over his face. "Oh! Online! I'm sorry. I didn't realize how that would look. I erased those Friday night when I got home because I'm handing over the mask and social media accounts to Amelia. I didn't want her to have access to all our private conversations. I saved them all."

My defenses melted, replaced with sheer relief and happiness. "You saved all the chats?"

He smiled a little. "Of course. You didn't think I'd save them? I saw you spit a piece of gum in the trash three weeks ago and I saved that."

I felt the look of disgust on my face before I realized he was joking. I hit his chest. We were good for each other. He saw through the crap other people couldn't and balanced out my driven personality with his relaxed one.

"Too soon?" he asked.

"No, you timed that one just right. Well, that and you are pretty charming."

He started to laugh but then realized what I'd said and his smile softened. "Really?"

I nodded. "Yes, really. You were right. I need people in my life."

"People?"

"You. I need you."

He smiled. "Same." His eyes darted to my lips. "I want to kiss you."

"Then do it."

"Is that a challenge?"

I shrugged, took a big sip of my drink, and walked away, trying not to laugh.

He cut me off before I'd made it two steps, wrapped one arm around my waist, and pulled me into a kiss.

"You are about to crush my Slurpee," I said against his lips.

Without pulling away, he took the Slurpee that was smashed between us and dropped it in the trash that happened to be to my left at the end of the row of lockers. I gasped and was about to protest loudly when he covered my mouth with his and pulled me closer.

2 MONTHS LATER

lay on my back in the lake, staring at the sky, which was a clear blue. Lazy clouds drifted by.

"Are you going to swim or play?" Jackson called from his perch on the shore. He held a stopwatch like he was an official trainer and sat in a big-armed camping chair. He was taking upon himself the training for my entry back into swimming. And he was taking it way too seriously.

I stood and tried to splash him but he had sat just

outside the splash zone. He was getting smarter. "Play," I said. "Why don't you come in with me?"

"Because you're supposed to be working."

I had taken a six-week break, doctor's orders. These last two weeks of swimming had been hard but good. It was hard in that I needed to condition my muscles again but I wasn't having the same pain in my shoulders that I'd had before. Apparently, the stress really had been messing with my swimming. The stress hadn't completely disappeared at home. We were all trying to find the right balance. The difference was that we were now talking about it.

"Leave her be," Amelia said from her towel beside him.

"If you can't beat the time, Moore, just say so."

I waded out of the water and onto shore. He knew I was coming for him but he just sat there with a smile on. I sat right on his lap. "I can beat the time. I just need someone to race."

"If you two are going to be gross, I'm leaving. I'm in mourning. I can't handle lovey couples right now."

"I'm sorry about DJ," I said.

She sighed dramatically. "It was never going to work out anyway. He was fourteen years older than me."

Jackson gave me his confused face.

"College years are like dog years," I whispered.

He still didn't seem to get it but, like he often did,

accepted that Amelia and I spoke our own language sometimes. He pushed me up and stood. "I'll race you, Moore, if you're prepared to lose again." He took off his shirt and jogged into the lake.

Before joining him, I glanced at Amelia. "You going to be okay?"

"I'm fine. I got another Heath Hall nominee. I need to research him and see if he's a good candidate for facing his supposed fear."

"Anyone fun?"

"Hadley, I can't tell you who. That would break my vow to the mask." She was taking her job seriously and I was happy. It had kept her busy since she and DJ called it off a few weeks before.

"Well, I have a boy to humble." I nodded toward the lake. "I'll be back after I finish beating him."

"Watch out, I hear he'll do anything to win," she said.

I laughed. "He will."

Jackson smiled at me as I walked into the water. "You ready to be taught a thing or two about swimming, Moore?"

I splashed him and he grabbed my wrists and pulled me into a hug.

"We're working, not playing," he said, his lips on my ear.

"Since when?"

He picked me up, spun me around, and threw me. Then he took off at a sprint toward the end mark.

I just laughed. Not even with a head start would he beat me. I dived under the water and swam as hard as I could. The water was cold, but it felt like endless possibilities as it flowed between my fingers. I felt free.

ACKNOWLEDGMENTS

To the little book that could. I love this book. I've loved it for years, since I first wrote it over six years ago. I thought it was going to be my fifth book in the world and here it is my thirteenth. There are so many reasons for this, reasons I didn't even realize at the time, reasons that now, looking back, make me so happy it took its time. So here's to patience, the little virtue that is always so self-righteously trying to teach me lessons. Sometimes it actually succeeds.

I love my readers! I love *all* readers, but maybe I'm slightly more partial to the ones that read my books. And by slightly, I mean I would hug all of you if I could. But seriously, thanks for all the support, whether this is the first book of mine you've read or the thirteenth.

My agent, Michelle Wolfson, is one of the best choices I've ever made. As a new, hopeful author, my gut told me this woman was the real deal—smart, witty, great instincts, driven—and I wasn't wrong. It's been almost nine years and I am grateful every day to have her.

To my editor, Catherine Wallace, thanks for everything. You've always been great at giving amazing advice while helping me stay true to who I am and I'm so grateful for that. And thanks to Jon Howard, Chris Kwon, Ebony LaDelle, Jacquelynn Burke, Meghan Pettit, and the entire HarperTeen team!

A huge thanks to my husband, Jared West. He is and always has been my biggest cheerleader. He's my first reader and always tells me he loves the book. Then, when subsequent readers suggest improvements (as they should) he says things like: What?! Why?! Or, Do you need me to fight them? His faith in me is unparalleled and I love him for it. And together we've raised some pretty cool humans. Skyler, Autumn, Abby, and Donavan, I'm so proud of you and thanks for being there for me and for each other.

I have some awesome friends. They've kept me sane this year. I love them all. I'm so lucky to be surrounded by caring, talented, amazing women. To name a few: Candice Kennington, Jenn Johansson, Renee Collins,

Bree Despain, Brittney Swift, Mandy Hillman, Emily Freeman, Megan Grant, Jamie Lawrence, and Elizabeth Minnick.

Last but not least, thank you to my family and support group: Chris DeWoody, Mark Thompson, Heather Garza, Jared DeWoody, Spencer DeWoody, Stephanie Ryan, Dave Garza, Rachel DeWoody, Zita Konik, Kevin Ryan, Vance West, Karen West, Eric West, Michelle West, Sharlynn West, Rachel Braithwaite, Brian Braithwaite, Angie Stettler, Jim Stettler, Emily Hill, Rick Hill and the twenty-five children (plus some of the children's children) who exist between all these people. These people are the reason I can write such big, close families!